CLOSE ENCOUNTER

"Captain Sacrette?"

Sacrette nodded to the strange vision two inches from his face. A vision that looked like it came from another planet. Tubes were jutting from where eyeballs would be found on a human being. Had he not recognized the device he might have fought. But he knew that would be useless. The grip of his captor held him pinned firmly to the ground.

"Yes. I'm Sacrette. Who are you?"

"I've been instructed to bring you back to the carrier, sir," said the voice.

"Like hell," Sacrette replied.

Then he saw the black muzzle of a weapon perched on the end of his nose.

———

Also by Tom Willard

Strike Fighters

Bold Forager

Published by
HARPER PAPERBACKS

STRIKE FIGHTERS

WAR CHARIOT

TOM WILLARD

HarperPaperbacks

A Division of HarperCollinsPublishers

This is a work of fiction. The characters, incidents, and dialogues are products of the author's imagination and are not to be construed as real. Any resemblance to actual events or persons, living or dead, is entirely coincidental.

HarperPaperbacks *A Division of* HarperCollins*Publishers*
10 East 53rd Street, New York, N.Y. 10022

Cover art by Attila Hejja

First printing: December, 1990

Printed in the United States of America

HarperPaperbacks and colophon are trademarks of HarperCollins*Publishers*

10 9 8 7 6 5 4 3 2 1

United States Navy Catapult Officers:
The men who make certain the pilot and aircraft are safely ready for launch. The men who kneel beneath the thundering aircraft; beneath the knife-like leading edge of the wing. The men who risk their lives during launch, eating the backblast from flaming afterburners, steadying themselves against the possibility of being blown overboard, being blown into the intakes or exhaust of waiting aircraft.

The men who die—whether of old age, or during launch—with the taste of JP-4 aircraft fuel in their mouth.

Marine Force Recon:
The unsung heroes of the fighting elite. Should their presence be known—their mission has failed!

My niece, Lindsay Ann LeDuc.

And, most especially, for *Lajos Hegy*, a young man I never met:
In December, 1989, during the bloody Romanian revolution, a group of school children chanting "Death to Ceaucescu! Down with Communism!" were approached by soldiers of the loyalist Romanian secret police—the Securitate—with their weapons aimed at the children.

Lajos Hegy placed himself between the children and the Securitate. His pleas to not harm the children were answered with a volley of gunfire.

Lajos Hegy was murdered . . .

The children escaped unharmed . . .

Carrying with them the memory of the price often required for freedom!

WAR CHARIOT

Prologue

0945. June 6, 1985.
Bandar Abbas Air Base, Iran.

CAPTAIN ABDULLARAN BAKR IGNORED THE FURNACE blast of heat waiting beyond the opening doors of the Alert Crew's ready room; he ignored the shrill note of the siren that became a long, steady drone.

He ignored the gnawing reality that this might be his last morning on earth.

His feet moved automatically, carrying him toward the red circle on the flight line where his Grumman F-14 Tomcat sat waiting, its engines already whining as the ground crew completed the initial firing of the twin TF30-P-412 afterburning turbofans.

He paused in his stride to stare in momentary sadness at the Tomcat, the last of the serviceable fighters left from the Shah's reign. And the war of attrition with Iraq.

He would be alone. Again.

Beneath the wings and fuselage, a ground crewman duckwalked from the port wingtip to the starboard wingtip, furiously removing red-flagged safety pins from the various rockets joined to the Tomcat.

As Captain Bakr climbed into the cockpit, the crewman pulled himself up the boarding ladder and removed two red-flagged safety pins holding the ejection seat firing mechanism in check. When he dropped to the ground his fist was filled with red flags, indicating that the weapons and seat were now armed for combat.

A slow, steady grin formed on the crewman's face; a grin that seemed infectious as Bakr's face suddenly filled with a broad smile.

Notions of death evaporated.

"*Allahu akhbar!*" The crewman mouthed the words over the roar of the engines as he straightened to attention and snapped a smart salute.

Captain Bakr returned the salute, glanced into the rear seat where his RIO, radar intercept officer, flashed a thumbs up.

"Prepare for take-off," Bakr said to the RIO, who was busy turning on the radar screen connected to the AWG-9 radar weapons system mounted in the nose radome.

In seconds, the Tomcat was rumbling along the blue-lined taxiway; in the front seat, Bakr "wiped out the controls," checking for aileron and rudder deflection. As he turned onto the main runway, the instant the nosewheel lined up on the centerline his left hand guided the throttles forward, through the four military power settings into Zone Five afterburner stage.

The twin engines shook the earth as the afterburners stormed to life, breathing a bright red tongue of flame from the engine exhaust nozzles as more than forty thousand pounds of thrust erupted where raw fuel was being injected directly into the engine exhaust.

In the cockpit, Bakr concentrated on the centerline while glancing quickly to the airspeed indicator. Outside, the ground began to rush by as Bakr slowly eased back on the control stick between his legs.

As the Tomcat broke ground, Bakr cleaned up the landing gear, took a deep breath, then hauled back on the stick.

The needle-nosed fighter shot straight up in a pure afterburner climb, then disappeared over the brown desert of southern Iran.

Battle Group Zulu Station, Persian Gulf.

Sixty miles from Bandar Abbas, Commander Boulton Sacrette, VFA 101 squadron commander, who was also the CAG, or commander of the air wing group assigned to the nuclear carrier USS *Valiant*, sat in his cockpit at Alert Five, buckled in and ready to launch. A-Five was boring, pain-in-the-ass duty, but necessary to provide responsive air cover should an intruder precipitate a hardening of the battle group defensive shield.

Painted in low visibility gray, his sleek F-18B Hornet, called the Strike/Fighter for its dual role as a fighter and light bomber, was locked into launch tension, the nose aimed straight down Catapult One.

A thin cloud of steam snaked from beneath the track, twisting upward toward the cockpit.

Another tandem-seated F-18B sat waiting in Catapult Two. The pilot, Lt. Commander Anthony "Domino" Dominolli, and his RIO dozed in the hot sun, tanning their faces with aluminum reflecting mirrors borrowed from the survival kit in their seat packs.

Sacrette was taller than most fighter pilots. Tall. Lean. And angular. Which was all the more apparent as he unbuckled the parachute risers from his torso harness and stood up in the cockpit.

As he slipped off his helmet, the sun shone against his dark hair. His eyes were blue, his face long and narrow; he looked the way a French-Canadian by way of Montana was supposed to look.

Sitting behind him in the RIO pit was Lt. Juan Mendiola, whose running name, or call-sign, was "Munchy," a name he earned in flight school when he was caught eating a candy bar at Angels eighteen while inverted.

Munchy was doing what he always did at A-Five.

"What's a four letter word for olive genus?" asked Munchy over the top of his crossword puzzle book.

Sacrette, whose running name was "Thunderbolt," said nothing. He was staring out toward the emptiness of the sea where the beige-colored outline of southern Iran lay scribbled against the horizon.

"Olea," Sacrette finally replied.

Seconds later the RIO was stumped again. "Five letter word for Muslim lords?"

Sacrette thought for a moment. "Singular or plural?"

"Plural."

As he started to answer, he was suddenly stopped by a strange sensation, a sensation that narrowed his eyes at the corners, giving him the hooded look of a cobra preparing to strike.

Quickly, he pulled his helmet back on, sat back in the cockpit and rebuckled himself into his Martin-Baker ejection seat.

"Get ready, Munch. Something's about to happen," Sacrette called through the oxygen mask that also housed his communication mike.

"What!" The Mexican-American RIO from East

L.A. replied. "How do you know?"

Sacrette grinned. "I'm a fighter pilot, son. I can smell action. And all systems are saying 'go.'"

No sooner had he finished when a voice came over the 5-MC loudspeaker above the carrier's flight deck.

"Launch the Alert Five." The voice of the air-boss boomed. "Launch the Alert Five."

Gripping the HOTAS, the hands-on-throttle-and-systems control stick between his legs, Sacrette adjusted the fuel to military power.

Unlike the heavier F-14 Tomcat, the Hornet didn't need afterburner power to launch from the carrier when in the fighter mode.

Thrust deflection shields rose behind the Hornets' tail section to deflect the blast from the engines, which, though burning at military power, could still sear the skin from a man's body.

A high, piercing howl filled the air; a steady rumble followed, signaling that the Hornets were primed for the crossbow-like shot from the flight deck.

"Fangs out!" Sacrette barked the fighter pilot's battle cry.

In the next instant, the catapult operator sitting at his console between the two bow catapults, returned Sacrette's sharp salute and pressed the catapult firing switch. Massive steam-powered pistons beneath the deck slammed forward along the track, hurtling the F-18 off the deck of the *Valiant*.

Sacrette felt twenty transverse g's slam against his body, pressing him deep into the ejection seat while activating his "speed jeans," the pneumatic pants worn over his flight suit. The jeans stopped the flow of blood rushing into his legs, preventing pooling in the lower extremities, which caused the pilot to lose consciousness during heavy g-force encounters.

Sacrette's eyes bulged; his vocal cords tightened, but he was able to function.

Calmly, he raised the nose as the airspeed built up.

In less than three seconds—and a distance of only two hundred feet—the Hornet had gone from its stationary position in the track, to three hundred feet off the deck of the carrier, riding on the carpet of fire now breathing from his twin GE F-404 engines.

Seconds later, the second F-18, flown by "Domino" Dominolli, the air wing exec, shot from the deck.

Throughout the carrier, sixty-five hundred crewmen exploded with a thunderous cheer as the Hornets were launched.

It was the newly commissioned nuclear aircraft carrier's first encounter with a hostile force.

In the red-light glow of the carrier's combat information center, or CIC, battle group commander Admiral Elrod Lord glanced at a console of electronic radar screens. He watched an imposing blip move closer to the transponder identification number of a target in the center of one of the screens.

In the background, a hysterical voice was speaking in broken English, radioing a Mayday signal.

"We are under attack by Iranian gunboats!" The voice of the Greek oil tanker *Knossus*'s captain screamed.

Lord took the microphone. "Be advised, help is en route, *Knossus*. Repeat. Help is en route."

Switching to the crypto communications channeled to Sacrette's fighter, Lord issued his order. "Wolf one

. . . Greek freighter under attack in Alpha sector. Have detected incoming aircraft. Proceed to Alpha sector. Interdict and assist. Observe all rules of engagement with aircraft."

"What about the gunboats?" Sacrette's voice shot back.

Lord didn't have to give the question a moment's thought. He replied, "Neutralize the threat."

Captain Abdullaran Bakr homed in on the rising column of black smoke twisting skyward from the turquoise surface of the Persian Gulf. He was now twenty-five miles from the Iranian coast. Thirteen miles beyond the internationally recognized border of the Islam state.

"Your brothers are to be protected from American intervention," Bakr's headphones crackled with the order from an Iranian officer speaking from the operations center at Bandar Abbas.

"Roger, Bandar." Bakr replied as his eyes roamed the sky. Nothing. Except the white sun above, the Gulf below.

"Tally ho!" Domino's voice broke radio silence. Automatically, he pointed past the HUD, the heads-up display mounted on the top of his instrument panel.

Smoke boiled from the Gulf. In the center, barely visible, was a nine-hundred-foot-long oil tanker.

Flames billowed beneath the thick, black smoke near the bow.

Darting around the tanker, small boats could be seen snapping toward the disabled ship, firing rockets, then retreating from the futile spray of small-weapons fire coming from the sailors at the tanker's topside railing.

"Boston whalers." Domino reported to the CAG, who was three thousand feet above, rotating in a TAC CAP, a tactical canopy above Domino.

Positioned in the Boston whalers were several Iranians manning a heavy machinegun at the bow, supported by port and bow grenadiers firing RPG-7 rocket launchers while more men fired AK-47 assault rifles from the stern.

"A regular potpourri of the Ayatollah's finest, Thunderbolt. They look like sharks attacking a floundering whale."

"Let's even the odds. Take the first run and hit them where it hurts the most, Dom. I'll cover, then follow you in with another slap on the wrist while you watch the top." Sacrette ordered.

"Wolf Two . . . fangs out!" Domino replied. He shoved the nose forward, increased airspeed and shot straight for the tanker's starboard bow.

At four-hundred miles-per-hour, Domino quickly reached to the left side of the instrument panel and pressed the A/G on the master arm panel, arming the air-to-ground rockets packaged in LAU-10 Zuni rocket pods slung beneath the fuselage.

"Hold tight," Domino breathed softly to the tanker.

When the gunsight "tipper" on the HUD settled onto a bevy of whalers, Domino's finger closed around the firing switch.

Four rockets ripple-fired from the Zuni pod, etching snake-like white contrails against the sky.

The rockets were followed by a burst from the Hornet's 20mm M-61A–1 multi-barreled Vulcan cannon mounted in the forward fuselage.

A river of red tracers burned a deadly path, appearing

to be in pursuit of the rockets.

The impact was tremendous.

A Zuni struck a whaler dead center, evaporating the boat and the eight unsuspecting Iranians manning the craft.

Three other boats were picked from the surface, then twirled violently on the cone of a rising column of water where the other three Zunis struck the surface. The sea appeared to open, then close around the whalers, swallowing the attackers in an instant.

Domino Zone-Fived the engines, hauled back on the HOTAS, then streaked for the sanctuary of the sky.

He could not hear the string of expletives shouted by the Iranian commander standing in one of the surviving Boston whalers.

"Kill him! Kill him! Kill the *shamoot* devil!" screamed Major Sabry Bakr, a naval officer of the Islamic Republic of Iran.

His seven-man crew stared wild-eyed, filled with fright, as the crazed officer fired his AK-47 at the fleeing American fighter.

The bullets touched nothing except the empty sky.

Then, one of his men shouted joyously. "Sabry, look!"

Sabry turned. Following the pointing man's finger, he saw their salvation on the horizon. *"Inshallah!"* He whispered. And he knew they were saved.

"Come," Sabry ordered. "Attack the tanker. Attack. Our brother has arrived."

Smiling, the men reloaded as an F-14 Tomcat bearing the green and red target circle of the Iranian air force appeared.

Major Sabry Bakr raised his binoculars and focused on the approaching fighter. Suddenly, a broad grin parted his lips beneath his thick moustache. He felt an overwhelming pride in seeing the aircraft.

Not because they were saved, but pride in recognizing the symbol painted in bold black letters on the beige nose of the fighter: the pilot's family moniker depicting the house of Bakr.

Captain Abdullaran Bakr would have gladly traded a kiss from the Ayatollah for a pair of long-range Doppler radar-guided Phoenix missiles. Having neither, he was forced to close ground on the two American fighters and fire one of his two remaining close-range infrared heat-seeking AIM-9L Sidewinder missiles mounted under the fuselage on each wing glove box.

"We're locked up! We've got two uninvited," Domino shouted into his microphone. The cockpit of his Hornet screeched from the lock-on warning sensors, indicating that his aircraft's heat source was being tracked by a pair of heat-seeking missiles.

"Going to ECM," replied his RIO, Ensign Adrian "Boz" Bozwell, while initiating the electronic countermeasures.

"Flares!" ordered Domino.

Boz fired the button on the flare dispenser. From beneath the fuselage, a string of magnesium flares left a white trail.

Flares were the best defense against a heat-seeking missile. Made of magnesium, which burns hotter than the engines of a fighter even at afterburner, flares could give the heat-seeker a distinguishable heat source, and the pilot a chance to survive.

The next step was to turn away hard, cranking between six and seven g's.

Seconds later, Boz shouted excitedly: "Echo!"

The echo of the Sidewinder exploding against the flare rippled through his radar onto the screen.

"Taking number two through the hoops," Domino shouted.

The most incredible feature of the Hornet was its ability to turn. The short, stubby wings allowed the Strike/Fighter to turn on a dime, often leaving the pilot with the sensation of still traveling in his previous flow of motion.

Coming out of the "bat-turn," named after the Batcar's rapid one-eighty-degree turns, Domino watched the Sidewinder fly harmlessly past.

Two thousand feet overhead, Commander Boulton Sacrette was about to test a theory he believed valid, a theory he called the David and Goliath theory of air combat.

The Iranian Tomcat was below him, and deadly. How deadly, Sacrette knew; he had commanded a Tomcat squadron before taking the reins as CAG of the newly deployed carrier.

The faster, bigger Tomcat could out-Mach and out-missile him in long-range fighting.

But up close, in the Mark One eyeball-to-eyeball duel of aerial combat, Sacrette knew who was the belle of the ball!

"Turn on the music, Munch. Let's find out if this bitch can dance!"

Munchy leaned back in his seat. He knew too well he was merely along for the ride.

He could visualize what Sacrette was doing in the

forward seat. He would switch the HUD display to the left digital display indicator. This would allow him to see the HUD on the DDI when he was flying into the sun.

Finally, the weapons system would be armed. The system selected was the one most loved by the Thunderbolt.

The modern fighter aircraft combined three elements: an aircraft, a weapons system, and a pilot. They all had to work together. In selecting the weapon, Sacrette thought in terms of the outline of a baseball diamond extending from his nose, what fighter pilots called the weapons envelope.

Should a flying threat be in the zone between home plate and the mound, the system was guns, since the target was close—about a half-mile and clearly visual.

From the mound to the outer edge of the infield was the heat-seeking missile range. This was generally up to approximately ten miles.

From the edge of the infield to the fences of the outfield, the long-range, stand-off radar guidance missiles were used. A pilot could shoot from roughly thirty to forty miles away with radar guidance, but not heat seekers, since the source wouldn't be accurately picked up by the missiles' sensors.

Unless the aircraft carried the deadly Hughes AIM-54 Phoenix. That million-dollar rail spitter could be fired from ninety miles.

That was the home run that cleared the fence, the stadium, and bounced off the hot dog vendor's head on the street outside Yankee Stadium.

Only one aircraft carried that puppy. The F-14 Tomcat. Which was what Sacrette was up against.

But he wasn't worried. If the Tomcat had a Phoenix,

he would have fired by now. The key to winning air combat was getting off the first shot. Which the Tomcat hadn't done.

That made the decision simple, and delectable.

Sacrette wouldn't use missiles. He would put his pride as a fighter pilot on the line.

Guns!

The aerial knifefight began with the Hornet sparking the Tomcat's radar, signaling the Iranian RIO with active radar emitters from the Hornet's Hughes AN/APG-65.

The screech alerted Captain Abdullaran Bakr that an enemy was approaching. Glancing up, he saw the Hornet descending at what he believed was Mach-plus. To go to wingswept and afterburner would give the Hornet a clear shot at his tail.

A clear shot with a heat-seeking missile.

Bakr had never seen a Hornet. He knew his Tomcat was faster. It was time to find out what all air combat came down to: the skill of the pilot.

Bakr adjusted his wings to zero-degrees sweep, and went into a tight turn.

"How many circles, my friend?" Bakr asked as he felt the g's nearly choke off his voice.

As though hearing, Sacrette countered with a hard right rudder, then slowed his airspeed, rolling out on the Tomcat's starboard wing.

"He's going for a one-circle fight, Munch," Sacrette said calmly, indicating that the Tomcat was coming nose-to-nose. "Let's see what he can do."

Instinctively, Thunderbolt felt the Iranian pilot's finger on the trigger as though he were joined to the fighter pilot telepathically.

A stream of tracers streaked from the Tomcat's nose.

During the precise moment of bullet flight, Sacrette dropped airspeed to the slow end, went to ninety degrees bank and hard left rudder, turning in a tight circle.

The bullets missed.

"You got him, Thunderbolt!" Munchy shouted as the Tomcat shot past off the starboard wingtip.

Smiling, Munchy flipped the Iranian RIO the bird. "Eat that, slick."

"He's going to the top." Sacrette saw the Tomcat's wings go to full sweep, lying back along the fuselage like some great eagle climbing for the heights. The nose came up; the afterburner breathed pure flame.

"Watch him. He's going for the scissors, Thunderbolt," Munchy shouted.

"Roger, Munch. Hang on. We'll clip his feathers." Sacrette Zone Fived the afterburner.

Both airplanes shot upward, with the heavier Tomcat drawing closer as the Hornet's afterburners allowed Sacrette to close ground in the pure afterburner climb of both aircraft.

"He's got to go over the top! Now, Thunderman, now. He knows we've got his six," Munchy shouted excitedly. He could see the Tomcat's six o'clock tail section; both afterburners made for a clear target. "Take him down before he starts drawing more airspeed and pulls away from us, Thunderbolt."

"All in due time, son. All in due time. We'll wait for his move," Sacrette replied. His deep blue eyes were shining.

Bakr was shaken by the miss; the Hornet was on his tail.

Sacrette saw the swept wings moving away from the

fuselage. "Get ready, Munch. He's going for the turn!"

Bakr felt the 9.4 g-force crushing his body as the Tomcat began a turning circle. *Now, you American bastard, I have you on the run*, he thought. Glancing out the cockpit, he smiled, knowing he would see the Hornet swing through the circle, exposing its vulnerable belly.

Bakr's finger closed around the gun switch. He would destroy the American in seconds.

Suddenly, the Tomcat's cockpit lit up with the screech of the lock-on warning. Panic filled Bakr for an instant; then he relaxed.

His eyes went to Heaven. His thoughts to Allah.

"Gotcha, Mohammad. I used to teach Tomcat maneuvers to the Shah's pilots," Sacrette breathed from his position behind the Tomcat.

Anticipating the Iranian's turn, Sacrette did what the Hornet does best: he executed a power-back one-eighty-degree turn, flying a short circle, knowing the Iranian would expect him to fly past the Tomcat.

Sacrette squeezed the trigger. A demonic river of bullets stormed from the cannon ports forward of the cockpit.

For an instant, the two fighters were joined by a solid line of fiery steel.

The Tomcat disintegrated. Tumbling end-over-end, the massive Grumman painted the sky with black smoke and molten red fireballs.

Moments later, the sky was quiet, except for the shriek of the Hornet, streaking toward the carrier.

Racing away from the tanker, Major Sabry Bakr had watched the air battle with a sense of pride that quickly turned to horror.

Tumbling from the sky, he saw his older brother's

plane engulfed by the flames of Hell.

There was nothing left but splintered remnants of the Tomcat as the whalers raced to where the Iranian fighter impacted against the turquoise water of the Gulf.

Swallowed by the water, his brother was gone. Nothing remained except the charred nose, floating listlessly on the surface. He would not have known it was a section from the forward fuselage except where the name of the House of Bakr was boldly painted. The letters were scarred, torn, barely visible.

Reaching down, he touched the hot metal; pain flooded his body. His dark eyes filled with tears, and there he swore his vengeance.

"I swear this oath, my brother. I will find this man, and all those responsible. I will avenge your murder... no matter the price!"

In the CIC, Sacrette's voice came over the radio as he spoke to Munchy.

"Your five-letter word for 'Muslim lords' is emirs. It's a title of honor given to descendants of Mohammad."

PART ONE: ███████ SUMMIT AT SEA

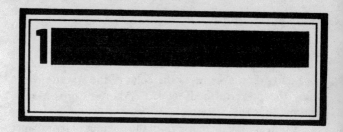

1900.
Marsaxlokk Bay, Valetta, Malta.

THE SURFACE OF MARSAXLOKK BAY CHURNED FU-
riously; sixteen-foot waves rolled in from the sea like
columns of charging tanks, slamming, pummeling, rid-
ding the surface of craft and men not built, or schooled,
to take the constant onslaught.

Fifty feet below the surface, beyond the jetty protecting the tiny harbor of Valetta, the fury was less fright-
ful, though just as deadly to those not trained for the
condition.

Sand rose from the bottom in cloudy cycles as the
energy raced toward shore from the depths. Finding bottom, it began a steady agitation as the wave energy collided with the energy returning to sea.

Storm surge.

Through this violence a lone diver appeared wearing
an electric blue wetsuit. He moved easily, pulled along
a few feet off the bottom by an orange-painted Farallon
diver propulsion vehicle shaped like an artillery round.

On his back he wore a twin set of 72-cubic-foot scuba
cylinders. His head was encased in a KMB diving helmet,
giving him the look of a man traveling through outer
space rather than inner space.

The face behind the glass-plated mask was richly tanned; high cheekbones framed a tapering, aristocratic nose and green eyes, eyes the color of the water enveloping the powerful body of U.S. Marine Corps Major Andrew "Deke" Slattery.

From above, the noise from the engines of patrolling surface craft beat a steady hum through the water, reminding Slattery of the constant vigil required both above and beneath the surface.

A vigil stood by two armadas to protect the two most important men in the world.

Men who at this moment were deciding the fate of the world.

Slattery couldn't see them, but he knew they were close. Three hundred meters away, beyond his range of vision, an anchor threaded to the sandy bottom from the bow of the Soviet luxury liner *Maxim Gorky*. In one of the luxurious conference rooms, the two leaders were meeting at this moment, surrounded by fighting ships and fighting men.

Two hundred meters behind him, another anchor line rose through the surface of Marsaxlokk Bay, to the bow of the USS *Belknap*. The flagship of the U.S. Sixth Fleet, the *Belknap* was the center of operations for the U.S. president.

Nearby, the Soviet guided-missile cruiser *Slava* lay in pitching anchorage, rocked by the unexpected storm systems colliding over the island of Malta. The *Slava* was the center of operations for the Soviet General-Secretary.

On the north side of Malta, a Soviet nuclear carrier Battle Group stood on station; at the center was the carrier *Kiev*.

To the south, the American Battle Group was on station; at the center was the nuclear attack carrier CVN 85, the USS *Valiant*.

The two Battle Groups sealed off the island; two armadas standing as bastions against any threat.

Except the threat of the elements, now pounding, forcing protocol changes aboard the *Gorky*, which was serving as the meeting place of what was being called the Summit At Sea.

"Red Cell One, this is *Belknap*. Be advised. Sonar reports target approaching your position from one-zero-five." The voice of the young sonar officer aboard the *Belknap*'s CIC crackled into Slattery's commo receiver.

"Roger, *Belknap*. Will investigate," Slattery responded.

Slattery rolled forward, kicked his powerful legs, and with a flick of his wrists pulled the DPV off the bottom while his grip closed around the power switch. Within seconds, he was propelling smoothly above the gritty sand bottom.

"Probably a Soviet diver," Slattery thought to himself. He knew Soviet commandos wearing neon red wetsuits were protecting the north side of the *Gorky*'s perimeter.

Slattery's unit, Red Cell Six, an elite Navy SEAL team, was protecting the southern side.

Trained to destroy each other, the two units were now acting in concert in an unusual form of aquatic military cooperation.

He checked his compass, and adjusted thirty degrees, taking a heading toward the approaching target.

Instinctively, from a pouch on his left leg, he raised a pneumatic speargun; on the point of the speargun, a

.12 gauge magnum powerhead was mounted.

"Red Cell team. Red Cell One. Proceeding on an outbound intercept heading of two-eight-five degrees. Close the gap and maintain positions. I'll find out what's on Ivan's mind. Probably their commander wanting to check our perimeter."

"Roger," five voices responded.

Slattery knew the Red Cell team would be deploying to take up the slack left in the perimeter by his departure.

"Horseshit visibility," Slattery mumbled to himself. Visibility was less than ten feet; sand swirled, captured in long, pulling undertows of wave energy racing into the bay, then retreating to sea.

He had traveled to a point directly beneath the *Maxim Gorky* when he saw the blur of a red wetsuit stir through the curtain of sand swirling along the bottom.

The blur was beginning to ascend, which brought Slattery to a sudden halt.

No military personnel were to approach the *Gorky* without authorization from both military powers.

Unless in case of an emergency.

Raising the nose of the DPV, Slattery aimed the vehicle toward the rising diver.

Within seconds he was pushing through the wake spilling from the Soviets' electrical motorized diver-propulsion-vehicle.

Reaching twenty-five feet, he glanced up, through the rush of bubbles bouncing off his faceplate.

In that instant, his eyes focused, and his heart skipped a beat.

"Christ," Slattery mumbled.

"Intruders!" Slattery's voice was crisp, unemotional. "We've got intruders inside the perimeter. They are heading for the keel of the *Gorky!*"

"*They!*" snapped the voice from the *Belknap*.

"Affirmative. 'They,'" Slattery responded.

Five feet ahead of Slattery, drifting over the electrical engine mounted in the rear of the Soviet DPV, three sets of diver fins trailed above the vehicle's wake.

Slattery squeezed the throttle as he used his body for a rudder to turn sharply to the starboard side of the ascending Soviet DPV; two seconds later he swung alongside the vehicle.

The fact that three divers were riding tandem on one DPV was suspicious enough; however, what the light mounted on his helmet revealed when the brilliant photoelectric beam framed the three divers confirmed his suspicions.

Especially the figure trapped between the top and bottom divers.

In the middle, the chalky face of a Soviet diver stared lifelessly through his face mask. Around his neck, a heavy wire was wrapped tightly, one end held fast in the grip of the diver on top, the other end held by the diver on the bottom, who simultaneously steered the DPV.

"Dagger! Dagger! Dagger!" Slattery shouted into his communicator, sounding the code word that meant eminent threat to the *Gorky*.

In the next instant, Slattery rolled off the DPV, knifing toward the three red-suited divers. It was a risky move, one not precipitated by the dead Russian or the two divers; he knew he could stop them before reaching the hull of the *Gorky*.

The move was necessary to stop the climb of the

DPV and the terrorist on top, who carried a satchel strapped to his body.

A type of military satchel Slattery recognized.

A satchel charged with explosives.

The living and the dead collided fifteen feet beneath the cruise liner.

Knocked from his grip, the bottom diver tumbled toward the sand, still gripping the dead Soviet diver.

Slattery took the top diver from behind; his hand flashed to his right knee. A long, sharp knife was drawn from a leg pouch.

"One terr is getting away," Slattery barked into his communicator. Looking past the diver in his grasp, he saw the second diver furiously releasing the dead Soviet. Within seconds, Slattery was alone, riding the back of the man strapped with the satchel charge.

Slattery's hand went to the throat of the diver; the sharp blade cut through the soft neoprene at a thirty-degree angle.

A slow, snaking trail of blood threaded from the puncture hole in the diver's neck. Turning the terrorist, Slattery saw two dark eyes suddenly appear in the light from his helmet.

Eyes filled with fright.

Eyes filled with dying.

A death throe followed. The terrorist's knees automatically snapped to the fetal position as the blade struck again, severing his spinal cord.

The light in the dark eyes faded; Slattery's green eyes burned like emeralds in banked coals.

Knowing the terrorist was dead, Slattery flung the diver aside and darted toward the bottom.

Suddenly, he slammed into something heavy. Rolling through a sea of bubbles, he saw the dead Soviet's body floating, as though drifting through outer space.

The air hose was cut at the second stage, near the mouth. Bubbles spewed wildly, churning the water into a cauldron.

Streaking past the dead Sov, Slattery again raced for the bottom. Feeling the surging tidal motion, he slowed, growing cautious. Carefully, he rotated a full three-hundred-sixty degrees. Scanning.

Nothing.

Turning, he checked his compass and started toward the south, toward the Red Cell team.

It was then that a flash of light off the bottom caught his attention.

Dropping down, he scooped through the sand. A medallion lay in the bright light from his helmet. He examined his find.

A round, flat medallion. Gold in color.

In the center was an emblem.

The emblem was in the shape of a circle. A circle formed by the joining of numbers.

The number seven.

2

THE *MAXIM GORKY* SAT IN WHITE SPLENDOR, ILLUMI-
nated by thousands of lights burning above deck and
from the hundreds of staterooms used by the Soviet del-
egation. Against the blackness of night, the ocean liner
shimmered like a fresh pearl lying in its shell.

On C deck, the plush red-carpeted hallways were
empty except for security guards stationed at thirty-foot
intervals. Each man stood at rigid attention, his eyes
locked straight ahead in that special misery known only
by those who have stood at parade guard. Dressed in
powder-blue berets and blue-and-white striped shirts of
the Soviet's elite *spetsnaz*, the paratroopers carried highly
polished AK-47 assault rifles; a walkie-talkie was attached
to their heavy, brown pistol belts.

Soft music drifted from the upper deck where the
General-Secretary was hosting the American president.

Corporal Boris Romanov was bored; his deep blue
eyes were tired, his shoulders were braced tightly, and
starting to ache. He wanted to stretch but he knew better; there was no telling who might be watching.

The staterooms were empty, except for one, room
312, two doors down from his station. One of the Soviet
delegates had suffered a mild case of ptomaine.

Ptomaine's ass!

Alcohol flu, Romanov sadistically wagered.

The bug was claiming more casualties than the *mu-jihadeen* sappers he had fought during the Afghan war. His hard demeanor broke momentarily as he thought of the foolish way many of the diplomats had embarrassed themselves since arriving for the Summit At Sea.

Security was tight aboard the *Gorky*. Then again, security was always tight where Soviets were concerned. That reality had honed their cunning to overcome adversity, in order to acquire what they needed. No matter what the risk.

The sound of laughter trickled from beneath the door of stateroom 312. Sounds always drifted into the hallways from the rooms. The doors were planed at the bottom to allow security personnel casual eavesdropping without being too obvious.

Privacy was one thing, he thought. Security was another.

He turned as an elevator opened at the end of the hall. A waiter appeared in a white serving coat and red slacks. On his lapel was the blue-colored identity badge.

Romanov watched the waiter approach. He was tall and dark-skinned, which immediately produced bile in the soldier's mouth. He couldn't see any dark-skinned man without remembering the *mujihadeen* soldiers.

The waiter was pushing a food cart. He moved slowly, purposefully, his dark face intentionally turned away from Romanov. The cart was square; trays of food were stored inside, heated by steam.

When the waiter stopped at door 312, he started to knock.

"One moment," Romanov ordered.

The waiter stiffened. Romanov stepped to the cart, where he motioned with a sharp jerk of his head. "Open the cart."

The waiter swung open the doors of the cart. The smell of food was nearly overpowering.

A quick glance, and Romanov jerked his head again. "Get on with your business."

The waiter bowed slightly, then knocked at the door.

The door opened, followed by the command of a loud voice ordering, "Enter."

The waiter and the cart disappeared.

Seconds later, Romanov heard a loud "pop." Then the sound of a woman's laughter.

Romanov shook his head. Light laughter could be heard from the other guards in the hallway. The soldiers were grinning.

Romanov whispered throatily to the guard thirty paces away, "The bastard is drinking champagne with his whore while we stand here with a hard-on."

The guard laughed.

From beneath the door of stateroom 312, the sound of another "pop" was heard.

This time there was no laughter.

3

1915.
Battle Group Zulu Station, south of Malta.

CAPTAIN BOULTON SACRETTE LEANED AGAINST THE coaming of the bridge; below, the windswept flight deck was nearly obscured by gale force winds turning the rain into slanting, stinging needles.

His attention was focused through a large pair of field glasses, on an F-18 Hornet approaching from the northwest.

"Come on, son. Put her in the trap. One shot. That's all you'll get tonight."

An arrested landing on an aircraft carrier cruising on calm seas during daytime was one of the most difficult tasks in aviation. A night landing on an aircraft carrier was considered the most hazardous landing in all of aviation. It was a little like placing a stamp on the floor, turning off the light, and having the pilot leap through the air, licking the stamp with the end of his tongue.

Making a night carrier landing in a storm, with the deck pitching, and the bow yawing from the corkscrew effect of the churning engine screws was next to impossible.

For the crew of the carrier, it brought moments of quiet concern as the pilot made his approach.

For the pilot, and the rear-seat RIO in the aircraft, it brought a deep, abiding faith in aircraft, training, personal ability, and at least for the moment, a closeness to God.

Lt. j.g. Ryan "Rhino" Michaels, the pilot of the Strike/Fighter, watched the horizontal lights of the Fresnel lens. The "Ball," as it was affectionately called by naval pilots, provided a visual slope indicator from its position on the starboard side of the rear deck, where the Hornet would approach to land.

Communication between Michaels and the landing signals officer on deck had ceased. Total concentration would be required for the final approach. The LSO, a veteran pilot, could only watch, and be ready to order a "go-around" should the Hornet appear to be off in its alignment.

Easing back on the power, Michaels felt the nose come up as he lowered the landing gear.

"Hold on, Gooze," Michaels called to his RIO. "The Ball lights are dancing around like a firefly in heat."

From the pit, Lt. j.g. Sean "Gooze" Thomas said nothing. He was busy placing his bet. RIOs share a universal belief where pilots are concerned: no matter who you've flown with before; no matter which pilot thought he was the best in the squadron or fleet, the one you were now flying with was the best.

It was that belief that kept them climbing into the backseat day after day.

At that moment, he was betting everything he had on Michaels. Which meant he was also betting on himself.

"I should have gone into submarines," Gooze said half-heartedly.

"What are you mumbling about?" Rhino snapped. The square landing lights of the carrier runway glowed like a Monday night NFL game as seen two miles away from the Goodyear blimp.

"Nothing! Just fly the aircraft and keep your mind on the line."

Rhino grinned at the carrier runway centerline, now thirty degrees beneath his nose.

"Knock off the chatter," the voice of the CAG barked over the radio from the carrier. "You're landing a $40 million airplane . . . not jumping out of a whorehouse window."

"Roger, Thunderbolt." Rhino replied.

"Give me a 'bad-to-the-bone' landing, son," ordered the CAG.

Rhino's hands tightened around the HOTAS. Beneath his dark brown eyes, and dark, thick mustache, his mouth spread into a broad smile.

"One bad-to-the-bone, coming up." Settling forward, Rhino eased back on the power slightly, adjusted his angle of attack, then released a long sigh.

"Hang on Gooze-man. One-eighty knots. Time to trip the lights fantastic."

What separated Rhino from most pilots was a simple and necessary belief, common among carrier-based fighter pilots: there was no doubt that he could make the landing. Since arriving aboard the carrier two weeks earlier he had rapidly established his rep as boisterous, swaggering, and afraid of nothing.

All the right ingredients for a first-class carrier-based fighter pilot.

"Wire three. Dead ahead." Rhino concentrated on the part of the deck where he would hit wire three, the wire all pilots tried to nail to prove they were macho.

"Take any wire you can get, Rhino," Gooze advised.

Before Rhino could respond, Gooze heard the power throttle back to idle; the air seemed to stand still. The wings waggled, and he held his breath.

"Christ! He's going for three."

The Hornet hit the deck with a crunch, grabbing wire three with the grappler as the roar of the engines again came to life.

A carrier landing was a near contradiction of purpose, once the wheels touched the flight deck. Automatically, the pilot shoved the throttles to full power, preparing for another take-off in the event that the aircraft missed the wire, or lost its grip on the wire, which was called a "bolter."

In the pit, Gooze released a long sigh as he heard the engines suddenly drop back to idle, and the g-forces slammed him into the ejection seat as the aircraft successfully held to the arresting system.

Sacrette took the microphone, and grinning, called to the young pilot. "Well done, Lieutenant. Well done."

Hanging the microphone up, Sacrette raised his coffee mug to the Hornet, which slowly taxied toward elevator two.

"He reminds me of a young, arrogant pilot I once commanded during Vietnam." Admiral Lord spoke from the starboard captain's chair.

"Who might that be, sir?" Sacrette turned to the admiral watching his reflection off the window glass of the bridge.

Lord was reclining; he wore a weathered, brown flying jacket. His face was slowly changing from the mask of concern that had clouded his features moments before, to a steady, cherubic glow.

"A young hotshot that flew with a monkey on his shoulder."

Sacrette chuckled. He hadn't thought about Martini since early that morning. He always thought of Martini, wondering if the chimp might have survived the SAM-missile explosion that destroyed his single-seat F-4 Phantom over the Red River Valley of North Vietnam.

"Best damned RIO I ever had. If only he hadn't drunk so much. He used to piss on my shoulder during the cat launch."

Both men laughed heartily. Sacrette couldn't remember the last time Lord had laughed so hard.

But their laughter lasted only moments.

A young ensign hurried from the CIC. He bent and whispered to Lord, "Admiral. Urgent message from the *Belknap*. We've got problems."

Lord shook his head and walked briskly into the CIC aft of the bridge.

"What's the problem, son?" Sacrette asked the ensign.

"Red Cell leader reports two intruders. The situation is now stable. The threat eliminated."

"Casualties?"

"One intruder killed. One Soviet diver killed. One intruder escaped. Red Cell leader is aboard the *Gorky*."

Sacrette looked back toward the flight deck. It seemed that all the elements, natural and unnatural, were lining up against the hope and promise the world prayed would be achieved at the Summit At Sea.

"What a clusterfuck night," he said.

4

THE WAITER STOOD AT THE PORTHOLE IN ROOM 312. The circular hole was stuffed with a blanket to block the howl of the wind that had blasted his face with stinging seawater when the window was opened.

From beneath the blanket at the rim of the porthole, the end of a rope dangled to the floor. The other end was fifty feet below, in the water beneath the *Gorky*.

The waiter checked his watch. His dark face burned with anger. He started to curse when the voice from a woman sitting on the bed cut the stillness.

"You fool. I should have known you and your comrades couldn't be trusted."

Idris Litvinov threw back her long blond hair. She wore a low-cut dress that barely covered her bulging breasts. There was nothing to cover the fury in her burning eyes.

"Quiet, woman," the waiter hissed. He was holding the rope, waiting for the sign from below.

He checked his watch. Jahlal should have reached his position under the *Gorky* with the satchel charge.

"They didn't make it to the keel. The plan is ruined. We have to get out of here. The guards will come and investigate if you don't leave."

She was checking her watch. Fifteen minutes had passed since the waiter entered the room.

She looked at the floor beside the food cart. Blood soaked the carpet beneath the body of a fat man lying on his side. His dead eyes stared emptily from beneath a single bullet hole in his forehead.

"The guards will come," she insisted again.

The waiter seemed to slump against the bulkhead beneath the porthole. "Perhaps you're right," he said defeatedly.

Litvinov jumped to her feet and threw a shawl around her shoulders. "Come. Help me with this pig."

She pulled back the bedspread; the sheets and pillowcases were made of silk.

The waiter grabbed the Soviet diplomat by the feet; Litvinov took his arms. The body was hoisted onto the bed.

"By the time he's found, we'll be ashore," she said. "Do you have my money and papers?"

The waiter nodded. "Your money and papers are at my apartment."

Litvinov nodded approvingly. "We'll go there. Then I'm through with you and your crazy fanatics."

The waiter's face darkened. "You have not completed your end of the bargain."

Litvinov's face twisted into a silent mask of rage. Words weren't necessary. The mask said everything.

The waiter stepped back. He had to be careful. One wrong move from this woman and his life would be ended by the guards in the hallway.

He said nothing. Instead, he went to the porthole. He pulled the blanket from the open window. A blast of air rushed through the opening like a tornado.

"What are you doing? Are you insane?" Litvinov was coming toward him, pulling the shawl tight around her shoulders to fend off the sudden cold.

She grabbed the waiter by the shoulder and spun him around. She saw his hand jerk toward her. There was the momentary flash of light off steel. Her ears began to ring; a sharp, stinging sensation erupted in her chest, just below the cleavage of her breasts.

Her legs went limp; she tried to speak but only gurgled. A rush of warm liquid filled her throat as blood flooded her mouth, then her nose.

"Inshallah!" the waiter whispered into her ear.

He turned the knife once, then held her, feeling her heartbeat against his chest until there was only one heartbeat between them.

Slowly, her dead body slid to the floor.

In the hallway there were shouts. The sounds of helicopters suddenly beat heavily in the storming sky beyond the porthole.

Guards could be heard going from room to room, kicking open the doors. There were only seconds to spare.

He stripped off his clothes, then tied the rope to the bed anchored to the floor.

Reaching to the food cart, he took a small vat of melted butter. He poured the butter over his shoulders and hips while walking to the porthole.

Placing a chair by the porthole, he leaned through the opening, working his right, then left shoulder until his upper torso was stung by the slanting rain.

The tightest fit was his hips, which he pulled through despite deep scrapes and gashes from the metal rim. He wanted to scream, but the pain was forgotten in his need to survive.

Finally, he was through the opening. He gripped the rope and began a long, painful slide down the side of the *Gorky*.

Reaching the water, he was nearly pulled beneath the hull as the surging action threw, then pulled his body against the sharp barnacles encrusted on the steel at the waterline.

Despite fatigue, dozens of razor cuts, and the fear of pursuit, he found the strength for one final effort.

Gauging the tidal surge, he waited for the water to throw him against the hull; then, he waited for the outgoing rush of water.

When the water started away from the hull, he lunged with all his strength, timing the release from the rope so that he would land on the leading edge of the wave.

He hit the water in a splash that went unnoticed. Quickly, without pausing to rest, he took a deep breath, rolled forward, and disappeared from the surface.

Fifty feet above, the barrel of Corporal Boris Romanov's AK-47 protruded from the porthole. From behind the rifle stock the young soldier was staring wildly into the stormy blackness of Marsaxlokk Bay.

He wasn't wondering why the Soviet diplomat was propped up dead on the silk pillows; nor why the beautiful blond woman, whom he knew was a KGB officer, was lying dead at his feet.

He was wondering where he would spend the rest of the winter.

In Siberia—Lubyanka prison.

Or in a cold grave.

5

Painted in low visibility gray camouflage, the Sikorsky SH-60B Seahawk struggled to descend onto the *Belknap* through the pouring rain. Wind shear pitched the nose wildly as the giant attack-helicopter was connected to the RAST cable, the recover-assist-secure-traverse system that enables a deck crew to winch a helicopter or Hawker Harrier into an aft securing station from a hovering attitude.

Admiral Lord and Captain Sacrette rushed from the Seahawk, hurrying head down through the blinding rain toward the quarterdeck.

Returning a boatswain's salute, Lord followed the sailor through the labyrinth of narrow, winding corridors until they reached the bridge.

Commander Brooks Washington, a tall, lanky black officer, rose from his exec's chair as Lord entered.

They shook hands and got down to business.

"Where's Major Slattery?" the admiral asked.

Before Washington could answer, a familiar voice came from the CIC.

"Right here, sir."

Lord and Sacrette turned to see Slattery standing in the bulkhead door; framed in a soft red wash of the CIC lights, the SEAL commander was still wearing his electric blue wetsuit.

"What's the situation, Major?"

Slattery shrugged. "Not much to tell, Admiral. The Sovs have quietly sealed off the *Gorky*. Apparently, they're running a low-profile search of the vessel. The captain of the *Gorky* reports nothing unusual."

Lord didn't look convinced. "What's your assessment?"

"Something was happening. Just what, I can't say." He held out the satchel charge.

Lord looked suspiciously at the explosive device. "That satchel charge couldn't have done any more damage to the *Gorky* than a mosquito on an elephant's ass."

Slattery nodded sharply. "On the outside. But, on the inside," his voice faded, leaving the innuendo hanging in the air.

"Yes. I agree."

Sacrette took the satchel charge. "An assassination attempt?"

"More than likely," Slattery replied. "I figure the terrs had someone aboard the *Gorky*. They only had one play. I believe the diver was going to run the satchel charge up a line fed from some point on the ship. Then, the person—or persons—unknown would plant the device somewhere near where the president and General-Secretary were meeting."

Lord released a long, slow sigh. "We dodged the bullet on this one."

"Barely," Slattery shot back.

"What about the dead terr? Any identification?" asked Sacrette.

Slattery reached into a pouch on his right leg. He

held up the gold medallion. "I found this on the bottom."

Lord examined the medallion. He began rolling the coin-shaped medallion through his fingers. "Any idea what this represents?"

Slattery shrugged. "None."

Sacrette looked closer at the medallion. "What makes you think the terr dropped the medallion? It could have been down there for days. Even months or years. Dropped by a tourist."

Slattery shook his head. "The bottom was moving too fast. It would have been covered over in seconds."

"Or uncovered," Lord pointed out.

Deke Slattery was a man who lived as much by instinct as fact. Lord and Sacrette had both come to trust the Red Cell Six leader's intuition. Intuition was what Slattery was basing his judgment on. Intuition and the odds.

"It belonged to the diver I killed, Admiral. The chances of that medallion being dropped at another time and suddenly appearing in that instant are too great."

Lord looked at the medallion again. "A circle made of sevens. It could mean anything. A design. Religious symbol. Hell, it could be nothing more than some special design by a jeweler."

"Doubtful," Slattery added cautiously. "There's something else. I found something interesting after I informed the *Gorky* that terrorists may be trying to come aboard."

"What did you find?" asked Lord.

Slattery took the medallion and laid it beside a computer keyboard. Carefully, he began turning the top of the medallion while holding the bottom steady.

The top screwed off, revealing an inner compartment. Inside the compartment, a fine powdery substance suddenly glowed from the red of the CIC lights.

"Poison?" asked Sacrette.

Slattery nodded. "I'm not going to be the one to give that powder a litmus taste test. But I'll wager it's poison."

"There's only one kind of assassin who carries concealed poison," Lord said emphatically.

"Fanatics," said Sacrette.

Lord nodded slowly. "Fanatics."

Slattery pointed at the medallion. "Which means we've got a new set of players in the international game of terrorism. Players who have the stones to try and take out the president of the United States and the Soviet General-Secretary under the tightest security on earth. Not to mention two naval battle groups, hundreds of spooks from both sides, and a raging storm."

Lord looked quickly at Slattery. "Do the Soviets know about the medallion?"

Slattery grinned as he shook his head. "I just bag them and tag them, Admiral. Foreign policy and diplomacy are somebody else's concern."

"Good." Lord appeared pleased with Slattery's decision. "I'll get this to our intelligence people. But first, what about the terr you killed?"

"He's in the cooler," said Slattery, pointing his finger belowdecks.

"Let's take a look at the gentleman," Lord ordered.

Two decks below, the three men entered the sick bay. A corpsman dressed in white snapped to attention as they entered.

"Where's the body?" Lord asked.

The corpsman led the trio to a room in the rear of the Sick Bay. Four small doors were set into the bulkhead wall. The corpsman unlocked one of the compartments and pulled out a body tray.

A figure lay on the tray beneath a white sheet.

Lord pulled back the sheet revealing the nude body of a young man.

"No more than twenty-five," Lord said acidly.

"Old enough, Admiral." Slattery pointed at the dead body. "Dark skin. Mustache. And there's something else you might find interesting."

Slattery lifted the body forward by the shoulders. Rigor mortis was already setting in, making the corpse move stiffly. Pointing at the upper back of the body, Slattery said, "He must have been a real zealot."

"Jesus Christ," Lord breathed heavily at what he saw.

The terrorist's back was deeply scarred; thick welts of scar tissue appeared like welding beads on his skin.

"Masochist is more like it," said Sacrette, who recognized the scars. Scars made by heavy chains. The type of heavy chains Iranian fanatics used to inflict pain on themselves to prove their loyalty to Allah.

"Iranian?" asked Lord.

Slattery's mouth pursed tight. "It's not without irony, you know."

"How's that?" Lord asked.

"Scotland Yard has traced the bombing of Pan Am flight 103 to Malta. The baggage used to carry the explosives was purchased from a shop here in Valetta. A man named Abu Talb, who is presently in jail in Sweden. Talb worked for Akmaed Jabril, the head of the PFLPGC, Popular Front for the Liberation of Palestine

General Command. The word is out that Jabril was hired by the Iranians to knock down the Pan Am flight in retaliation against the *Vincennes*'s attack on the Iranian Airbus over the Persian Gulf."

Lord pointed at the body. "He's not Palestinian."

"No, sir. He's Iranian."

Sacrette was beginning to understand. "Which means the Iranians are doing their own dirty work. Not using the PLO."

"That's correct," said Lord. "Central Intelligence has warned the president and secretary of defense that a group of fanatical Iranians, operating outside the authority of the Iranian government, may be carrying out their own form of reprisal against the United States. The fact that flight 103 comes up again, and here in Malta, is not surprising."

Sacrette thought about the admiral's comments for a moment. Then, he said very carefully, "The captain of the *Vincennes* was attacked in San Diego last summer. A car bomb nearly killed his wife."

Lord threw the sheet over the body. "At least this time, they failed."

"Thank God for small miracles," said Sacrette. "I don't want to imagine what this would have done to east-west relations if that satchel charge had gone off aboard the *Gorky*."

"You're right. But, at least one thing appears certain," said Lord.

"What is that, Admiral?" Sacrette shoved the body tray into the cold storage department.

Lord started walking away. "The Soviets are clamping a lid down on this incident. I suspect we'll do the same. Too much embarrassment. Too much at stake."

Sacrette looked at Lord in bewilderment. "You mean it never happened?"

As Lord walked into the corridor outside the sick bay, his words were almost imperceptible. "That's correct, Captain. It never happened."

PART TWO: THE *HAFIZA*

6

Monastery of Kims. Iranian desert.

THE MUEZZIN, WHO WAS A CRIER TO THE FAITHFUL, made the slow, arduous climb up the stone steps five times a day to the minaret, where his powerful, penetrating voice spoke clearly through the desert sky south of Abadan.

"God is most great. I testify that there is no God but Allah. I testify that Muhammed is God's Apostle. Come to prayer, come to success. God is most great."

From spartan cells within the walls of the mosque below, seven old men rose from their sleeping mats. Quickly, they rolled their mats into tight rolls, placed them in the corner, then stepped into the narrow hall.

They said nothing. Each walked slowly toward a winding staircase that led from the cellar to an ablutions room where they completed the obligatory washing before prayer.

When washed, they walked from the ablutions room, through the courtyard past the central fountain to the main prayer room.

The main prayer room was seventy-five feet wide, fifty feet long. Above the center of the room was a dome; the inside was painted blue. The outside, seen from a distance, was prominent, painted in gold.

Supported by ten marble pillars, the dome looked down upon the prayer room.

In the middle of the west side of the prayer room, on the side facing Mecca, is the *mihrab*, a semicircular recess every worshiper must face.

The seven men knelt facing the mihrab. Facing toward Mecca.

Hakim, the Imam, read the morning service. When finished, he motioned to the six others, all of whom were mullahs. Slowly, the old men moved to the center of the room, where they sat on the cold floor in an enclosed circle.

With a clap of his hands, Hakim signaled a tall bedouin standing guard outside the main prayer room.

The bedouin entered. In one hand he gripped a halberd, in the other, a leather rope. At the end of the rope was a man. A man who was stripped naked.

Sunrise began to come fast over the desert; the black night turned purple, then red, finally gold as the sun rose on the eastern horizon.

". . . come to success . . ." The words from the Koran rose from the group of seven, as though to challenge his existence.

"Why have you returned?" asked Hakim.

The seven old men waited for an answer; long beards flowed from their weathered faces into the heavy robes covering their frames.

Finally, the naked man spoke from the center of the circle.

Sabry Bakr sat on his knees facing east, where the morning sunlight flowed through an open window, capturing his naked body in a flood of golden light. His words came slowly, carefully chosen so there would be no denial of his failure and humiliation. No denial.

"I have failed Allah. I have failed the *Hafiza*. I have failed my sacred vow."

Hakim nodded slowly. "You failed to kill the American president and the Soviet General-Secretary. Two of our clients' worst enemies. The opportunity will never come again."

Sabry said nothing.

Hakim continued. "Failure is rewarded with death. You should know. You reported the death of your two servants. One was killed by the Americans. You killed the second man for failure. You killed the Soviet woman for her failure. Why have you—a failure—come to the *Hafiza*, if not for death?"

It was true, he reminded himself. He had failed. The only glimmer of pride left in his body was remembering the diver who had dropped the satchel charge and fled. Sabry found him later that night after his escape from the *Gorky*.

And the Russian KGB woman dying at the end of his blade in Malta.

Now, his life sat in judgment.

"What is your sacred vow?" asked Hakim, leader of the *Hafiza*.

"To prey upon the devil worshipers of the east and west. To punish. To purify. To avenge the wrongs against Islam in the name of Allah."

From the circle, Hakim's arm flashed toward Bakr. A long, tapered whip snapped across his back, leaving a single, thin streak near his spine. The dark skin was split; white tissue beneath the cut quickly turned red with blood.

Sabry did not cry out in pain. It was forbidden.

Hakim passed the whip to the old man sitting to his left.

"To whom do you owe your allegiance? Your life?" asked the second old man from the circle.

"To Allah, and His instruments of the path to purity. The *Hafiza*. Guardians of the Koran."

The whip cracked again off Sabry's back. The muscles quivered where his flesh was again rent by the razor tip of the leather whip.

"What do you seek from the *Hafiza*?" asked the old mullah sitting beside Hakim.

"Redemption," Sabry replied.

Another crack of the whip. More questions followed, allowing the fanatic to carefully purge his system of the failure.

Seven questions were asked. Seven lashes of the whip stung Bakr's back, leaving the painful reminder that the *Hafiza* did not tolerate failure.

"You seek redemption," Hakim said in a flat voice.

Sabry Bakr lay prostrate, facing the east.

Hakim looked up from the circle. Standing beside the window was the tall bedouin. His face was wrapped tightly with a red and white kaffiyeh, leaving only his eyes exposed. Hot, flaming eyes devoid of pity, of compassion.

In his hands he held a sixteenth-century halberd. The ax-like blade and steel pike mounted on a six-foot pole gleamed as the bedouin stepped to the circle and thrust the pike within inches of Sabry's head.

Sabry crawled forward and kissed the cold steel of the lance.

A slow mumble began among the old men in the circle. Heads bobbed; whispers passed advice to the leader of the *Hafiza*.

Finally, the decision had been made.

"You may seek your redemption," said Hakim.

From inside his robe Hakim removed a file folder. He carefully opened the folder, revealing two dossiers. Attached to each of the dossiers was a photograph. He spent the next few minutes carefully examining the dossiers, making certain to match the photographs with the particular historical background of each of the two names enclosed.

The faces and histories were familiar; he had spent hours learning all there was to know about the two men. Hours. And a great deal of money.

When satisfied, he placed the folder on the floor in the circle and stood.

"Bring them to the *Hafiza*," Hakim told Sabry Bakr. "From our justice, you will find the path to your redemption."

Hakim stood and walked from the room. The others in the circle followed. Their leather sandals beat a steady rhythm across the stone floor; a rhythm that could be heard as they walked through the ancient archway, followed by the bedouin.

When he was certain they were gone, Sabry reached for the folder. He went to the sunlight of the window. Below, a courtyard was enclosed by three massive walls extending from the Mosque of Kims, a Shiite monastery older than the copper-colored village lying in the distance.

He read the folder carefully, making special notation of the pictures attached to the dossiers.

He read with little interest the dossier of the first man; a man he had never seen, but knew was sworn to bring to the judgment of the *Hafiza*.

It was the second dossier he read with extreme interest, feeling his pulse begin to quicken as the history of the man began to join their lives in the present, just as they had once been joined in the fire of the past.

Tears flooded his eyes; anger swelled within his chest until he thought his lungs would burst.

A loud, painful scream followed and he fell to his knees. "Allah. Be praised. In Your infinite wisdom you have given me Your blessing. I will not fail."

Sabry Bakr stared hatefully at the folder; at the photograph on the second dossier.

A *Navy Times* photograph depicting a naval flight officer sitting in the cockpit of his fighter plane.

Beneath the photograph was the painful truth joining the two men. The redemption of Sabry Bakr. The caption read:

CAG Sacrette claims first kill for USS Valiant!

7

SPIRITS ABOARD THE USS *VALIANT* HAD SAGGED TO AN all-time low; the expected return to port from special assignment at the Summit At Sea had been followed by an early morning weighing of anchor and flank speed toward the Suez Canal.

The Battle Group passed through the "Ditch," as the Canal was called by Navy personnel, and proceeded through the Red Sea, the Gulf of Aden, along the coast of Southern Yemen and Oman until reaching the southern entrance of the Persian Gulf.

Scuttlebutt was running at an all-time high; the crew knew relative peace had returned to the Gulf, which caused them to wonder why the Battle Group was now moving northwest off the coast of western Iran.

Not the Panama Canal Zone. All eyes and ears of the men of the Battle Group were focused on the Canal Zone where twenty-four thousand American troops were waging a deadly street war against Panamanian Defense Forces loyal to self-appointed General Manuel Noriega, the narco-dictator who had tweaked the United States' nose for more than two years.

Noriega was on the run, hiding in the jungles while

troops of the 82nd Airborne, 196th Light Infantry, and U.S. Marines were in hot pursuit.

While the USS *Valiant* steamed into peaceful waters.

Why? The question was on the lips of every man in the Battle Group.

Only one man in the Battle Group knew the answer.

On Christmas Eve, that man knew it was time to share the information with the Battle Group commanders.

The admiral's mess was chosen by Admiral Lord as the briefing room; seated at a long table were the fourteen captains of the Battle Group ships, including CAG Sacrette.

Admiral Lord rose from his chair at the head of the table. He wore his white uniform, as did the other officers.

"Gentlemen. I'm sure you're wondering why we have been dispatched to the Persian Gulf and not to the Panama Canal Zone," Lord began the briefing.

A low grumble drifted through the men seated in the leather chairs facing the admiral. Christmas leaves had been cancelled for officers and enlisted personnel, making the captains unpopular with their men. Which, in turn, resulted in making the admiral unpopular with the captains.

Lord took a pointer and turned to a large map of the Middle East. The pointer touched a spot southwest of Baghdad, Iraq.

"This is the Iraqi space research center at Al-Nasra. Intelligence sources have determined the Iraqis are preparing to test-launch a three-stage surface-to-surface missile with a range of approximately twelve-hundred-fifty miles."

A high-pitched whistle rang out.

Lord looked at the captains. "My feelings exactly. And the feelings of both the president and the Soviet General-Secretary."

"Is that where the information came from, Admiral? From the Soviets?" asked Joshua Wharton, captain of the guided-missile cruiser *California*.

Lord avoided the answer directly, choosing to say only, "I'm not privileged to the source. Only the information. Which the president is acting upon in good faith."

"What about the Soviets?" another captain asked. "What's their part in this?"

"The Soviets have moved their Kiev Battle Group to a station off Cyprus. They are monitoring Iraqi activity from the north. We will monitor from the south."

"Is that our mission? To monitor? Nothing more?" asked the captain of the nuclear ballistic-missile submarine USS *Will Rogers*.

Lord put down the pointer. There was something in his movement that suggested he didn't like the situation any more than the captains. Something that suggested it was time to accept the situation for what it was, and stow the whining and bellyaching in order to get down to business.

"I don't think I have to remind you gentlemen of the threat something like this poses for the security of the Middle East. The entire world, for that matter. If the Iraqis do have missile capability of the range reported, they could deliver packages to all of the Middle East, including Greece, Cairo, Israel, Iran, and the southern part of the Soviet Union."

"Packages?" asked Sacrette. "Are you suggesting

nonconventional nuclear packages?"

Lord nodded. "It's no secret the Iraqis have advanced considerably in the field of nuclear science. You may recall Israel's attack against an Iraqi nuclear power plant the Israelis suspected was being used for developing nuclear weaponry. The same fear has again manifested itself. Only now it's heightened by the possibility the Iraqis may have long-range delivery capability. Those two capabilities could reconstruct the nuclear complexion of the entire world. If that's the case, we have to know with certainty."

An uncomfortable silence settled over the group of commanders. Each man was momentarily lost in his own thoughts, mentally analyzing the deadly nuclear gameboard that could change dramatically with the addition of another player.

An unpredictable player.

"For all practical purposes, the Battle Group is in the Gulf on a good-will tour. The *Valiant* will make its first port-of-call tomorrow in Kuwait. Anchorage will be in the port of al-Ahmadi, south of Kuwait City, the capital. A reception and dress dinner will be held tomorrow night at Al-Seif Palace in Kuwait harbor. We will be the guests of the emir, and the U.S. Ambassador to Kuwait."

"When you say 'we,' to whom are you referring, Admiral?" asked Sacrette.

Lord swept his arm at the gathering of captains. "Every man in this room. With one exception."

Captain Wharton, a tall, handsome man in his late forties, pointed at the map. "Has intelligence estimated when the Iraqis intend to launch the missile?"

Lord shook his head decisively. "No. Which means we have to be prepared to track and monitor on a moment's notice. All personnel assigned to tracking will remain aboard ship. Nonessential personnel are authorized shore leave for twenty-four hours."

"What if the Iraqis are successful?" asked Sacrette.

"I have been instructed by the chairman of the Joint Chiefs that in the event of a successful launch, our Battle Group and the Kiev Battle Group are to have prepared a contingency plan. A plan that will be a joint American-Soviet operation."

"Joint operation? With the Russians!" Sacrette asked incredulously.

"That's correct, Captain Sacrette. The plan will be an air strike."

"Air strike? The media will go nuts over that notion."

Lord shook his head to the CAG's suggestion. "That's why it's a joint venture. If we—or the Sovs—hit the complex, world opinion would rock from either side of the dividing line. If we do it together, we can keep our allies in line. Only the Chinese will scream, but since Tianamen Square, not many people care what they say. Especially in the United States."

Sacrette nodded. "Makes sense, I suppose."

"Since you are commander of the air wing, you will coordinate the contingency plan with your Soviet counterpart. You will prepare to depart immediately for the Soviet Battle Group where your counterpart is awaiting your arrival."

Sacrette began to feel an uneasiness thread through his body. An uneasiness he feared would be answered by his next question; the answer to which he suspected he already knew.

"Who is my counterpart, Admiral Lord?"

Lord took a deep breath. His reply came without emotion. "Major Sergei Zuberov!"

Sacrette's blood turned to ice water. "You can't be serious, Admiral."

Lord looked sternly at Sacrette. "Captain, you will harness your personal feelings and conduct yourself in a professional manner."

There wasn't a single man seated at the long table who wasn't aware of the personal feud that existed between Sacrette and the Soviet officer.

Both men were locked in a death-feud that had begun over the skies of Lebanon years before, when Sacrette lost one of his men to a Syrian fighter flown by a Soviet pilot.

Naval intelligence later revealed that the Soviet pilot was the son of the Soviet Air Marshal commanding southern defenses for the Russian Air Force. Soviet Air Marshal Lieutenant General Pietor Alexandreyevich Zuberov.

Major Sergei Zuberov.

8

"WHAT THE HELL DO YOU EXPECT, THUNDER-bolt?" asked CPO Desmond "Diamonds" Farnsworth. "Relations with the Sovs are changing on a daily basis. Hell, for all practical purposes, the eastern bloc has fallen. The Warsaw Pact is nothing but an army on paper. NATO will probably be next. The troops will be coming home."

The chief was sitting on a boarding ladder beside a McDonnell Douglas AV-8B Harrier II short take-off, vertical-landing (STOVL) attack aircraft. Since the Harrier could take off and land vertically, several were deployed through the Battle Group, giving the larger ships within the BG an added onboard attack aircraft capability.

The Harrier was on elevator three in the massive two-and-one-half acre hangar deck beneath the flight deck of the nuclear carrier. The occasional thump of a landing aircraft shook the air as did the intermittent high pressure sound of the steam-driven catapult launching aircraft into the sky.

Rows of brightly polished F/A-18 Hornets from VFA 101 were parked side by side, their wings folded at the wing-folding joints to allow maximum use of limited space to park the more than one hundred airplanes of the air wing.

As the CAG, Sacrette commanded all the planes; those parked belowdecks, on the flight deck, and those on routine air patrol protecting the Battle Group.

An awesome responsibility. But, he thought to himself, no more awesome than the newest challenge affecting his life.

Farnsworth, a short, powerfully-built black man, was the maintenance chief of VFA 101, and a close friend of Sacrette's. They had known each other since Vietnam when Farnsworth, a SEAL at the time, rescued Sacrette near the DMZ after the aviator's F-4 Phantom was shot down by a SAM missile.

This allowed Farnsworth a certain latitude with the CAG; one that included candor.

"You have to put your personal feelings behind you on this one, Thunderman." Farnsworth was buckling the Martin-Baker 9D ejection seat parachute lugs into the capewells of Sacrette's torso harness.

Sacrette didn't appear interested in the advice, though he knew the chief was probably right. Chiefs generally were. That's why God made chiefs. They were the exceptional personnel that kept the navy functioning.

Sacrette shook his head. "Some things can't be changed, Diamonds. No matter how important."

"I know you don't like the Russian son of a bitch. But you don't have a choice. You can't go aboard their carrier hauling a bomb rack full of attitude. The brass will eat your ass up. You got to work with him, not sleep with him."

Sacrette grunted. "Maybe I should send you in my place. You're a vodka lover."

Farnsworth shook his head. Beads of sweat rolled down his shaved pate. His deep brown eyes twinkled.

"I hear they bring women on their cruises."

Sacrette laughed. "They probably have hairy legs."

Farnsworth closed the capewell. Certain the lugs were locked in tight, he slapped the CAG's shoulder. "Ready to roll."

Sacrette checked his watch.

1600.

Farnsworth climbed down the ladder, then saluted smartly. Sacrette returned the salute. Brown-shirted plane captains stood at each wing as the whine of the elevator filled the inside of the flight deck.

All activity seemed to stop for the moment. Hundreds of mechanics paused from their jobs to watch the elevator rise into the air, then disappear onto the flight deck.

The sky was clear; clouds were thin, mostly cirrus at thirty thousand feet. The sun was hot, searing, as usual in the Gulf.

The Harrier was guided to an area near the bow catapult. The launch crew did nothing except watch since the launch would be vertical, not catapult.

Sacrette lit the powerful Rolls Royce Pegasus vectored-thrust turbofan engine, bringing to life more than twenty thousand pounds of thrust.

He set in ten degrees of wing flaps and adjusted the swiveling forward exhaust nozzles to sixty degrees. Funneling engine exhaust through the nozzles was how the Harrier would get its vertical lift thrust.

"Clear for take-off, sir," the voice of the air boss came over the radio.

The principle of the Harrier was simple: lift over drag, thrust over weight, as with all aircraft. In the case of the Harrier, this was done vertically, rather than longitudinally. Venting the engine thrust downward made the aircraft rise slowly; simultaneously, the aircraft could ease forward, building airspeed.

Lift over drag. Thrust over weight.

In one helluvan ass-tightening few seconds!

Sacrette eased forward on the engine throttle lever until the heavy Harrier began to quiver. As the thrust built up, the jet fighter slowly lifted vertically off the deck like a giant condor. The rear thruster nozzles vented power to the aft, giving the Harrier forward drive while the downward thrust from the forward nozzles made it rise. Within seconds the aircraft was moving forward in ground effect, gradually building airspeed in a slow, steady departure from the carrier deck.

As the airspeed built, the vertical swiveling nozzles were gradually decreased in angle to the neutral position until the Harrier was flying straight and level. All thrust was now venting along the longitudinal axis.

The process took only seconds before the aircraft was winging west, climbing at four thousand feet-per-minute en route to Angels twenty-four.

Glancing down, Sacrette could see dozens of tiny scribbles against the turquoise water of the Gulf south of Bubiyan Island near the east coast of Kuwait. White signatures etched slow, lazy scrawls into the water where lateen-rigged dhows plowed the surface as they had for centuries.

Sacrette noticed one particular dhow was off the normal sailing route through the channel dividing Bubiyan and the ancient island of Failaka, where Greek trading ships used to stop more than a thousand years before.

The dhow was on a southwesterly tack, not more than ten miles from the great aircraft carrier USS *Valiant*.

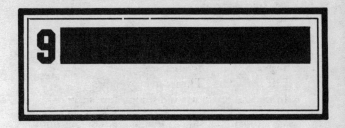

9

SABRY BAKR WATCHED THE VAPOR CONTRAIL OF AN American fighter plane climb to where the blue of the sky turned white against the heat of the burning sun. In a matter of seconds, the aircraft was gone.

The modern was now vacant from the ancient.

Much like his clothes. He wore a long flowing robe; a white *hatha* was wound tight around his head, revealing only his face.

When the white sand of the bottom gleamed beneath the turquoise water, Sabry dropped over the side of the dhow and began walking toward a small promontory on the island of Failaka. On the beach, waiting less than two hundred meters from the shrine of Al-Khidr, stood a tall woman.

A sentinel island guarding the bay of Kuwait, the most notable feature of sparsely-populated Failaka, is the shrine of Al-Khidr. Named for a Muslim saint whose spirit is said to stop in Failaka on Wednesday and Saturday during its journey between Mecca and Basra, the shrine is popular among Shiite women for its fertility powers. To the child-barren followers of Ali, superstition promises a visit to the shrine on one of these days will be rewarded with the birth of a child.

She was young and tall, with long black hair braided in tight coils piled onto the top of her head. Her oval eyes seemed to be examining him closely as he stepped from the water to the beach. Reaching to her throat, she touched a medallion hanging from a gold chain.

Sabry touched a similar medallion hanging from his neck. Both medallions were inscribed with the same insignia.

A circle composed of seven numbers.

The number seven.

10

2000.

At twenty-four thousand feet the Mediterranean lay dark beneath the nose of Sacrette's Harrier; the sky was still light at the western rim where the sun was beginning to fade into blackness.

Reaching to the instrument panel, he tuned in the radio frequency given him before departure from the *Valiant*, then spoke slowly and evenly into the microphone.

Don't want the bastards to misinterpret, he reminded himself.

"To the Soviet aircraft carrier *Novorosiysk*. This is Captain Boulton Sacrette. United States Navy. Request permission to come aboard."

A short silence followed, then he heard the near-perfect English reply from the Soviet communication officer aboard the Russian carrier. "*Novorosiysk* to American Navy Captain Sacrette. Permission granted. Landing two-seven-zero. Wind from two-six-zero at eight knots."

The *Novorosiysk*, the newest in the Kiev class of Soviet aircraft carriers, lay off Sacrette's port wingtip. He would have preferred flying his F/A-18C Hornet Strike/

Fighter, if for no other reason than to show the Russians what the newest American carrier-based fighter-light attack bomber looked like up close. However, landing would have been a problem.

The Soviet navy only has two carriers beside the *Novorosiysk*, the *Kiev* and *Minsk*, all of which are short 'jump deck' carriers. None are capable of receiving, or launching an aircraft type of the F-18 or F-14 Tomcat.

The Russian navy's exclusive carrier-based attack fighter is the Yakovlev Yak-38 Forger, the Soviet Union equivalent of the Harrier.

Which was why Sacrette was flying the stripped-down Harrier. All ordnance was absent; anything that could be considered classified was back on the *Valiant*, safely tucked away from probing Russian eyes. He was flying the basic Harrier, whose plans he figured were probably stolen by the Sovs to build their Yaks.

Sacrette approached low, noting the standard complement of twelve Yaks parked near the island, the superstructure rising from the flight deck.

Through the darkness he saw the light of a landing officer signaling him to approach for landing.

When the wheels of the Harrier touched down, he chopped the power and popped the canopy. Rising from the seat, he saluted as an officer approached wearing full dress uniform.

Swinging over the side, Sacrette came to attention as the Russian Battle Group commander stopped and waited for Sacrette to climb down from the Harrier.

"Welcome aboard the *Novorosiysk*, Captain Sacrette," said Admiral Yuri Galenin.

A short, stocky man, Galenin had a cherubic face; deep blue eyes smiled warmly.

In keeping with naval traditions, the two men exchanged salutes, handshakes, and small gifts.

Galenin handed Sacrette a small wooden box. There was a wry smile on the Soviet's face. "I understand your last visit to Cuba—and your hasty departure—precluded you from returning with one of the few treasures of Comrade Castro's paradise."

The rich smell of Cuban cigars drifted from the box.

Sacrette grinned. He wasn't surprised the Russians knew about his crash-landing near Cuba three months earlier. Flying a top-secret version of the night-configured F/A-18, he and Farnsworth had gone down near the Communist island and evaded the Cuban army in their harrowing return to the *Valiant*.

But not before sinking the Hornet in a deep blue hole. The plane was later recovered in a covert salvage operation beneath the Cubans' noses.

"Yes, sir. It was a nervous trip, Admiral. Perhaps I'll get the opportunity to go back someday."

Galenin laughed. "Perhaps. The way the world is changing so rapidly, you may get there before I do."

Sacrette handed Galenin a cylindrical tube containing a fifth of scotch. "Admiral Lord sends his compliments."

Galenin smiled affectionately at the tube. "Aberlour. My favorite. Hopefully, *perestroika* and *glasnost* will improve the quality of Soviet drinking as it improves the quality of Soviet international relations."

Sacrette nodded sharply in agreement. "Hopefully."

"Let us hope your optimism extends beyond the subject of fine liquor and cigars, Captain Sacrette." The voice came from a figure walking from the island onto the flight deck.

A voice Sacrette would know anywhere. A voice he heard in his dreams. The voice of a man taunting a young American pilot as his aircraft disintegrated over the skies of Lebanon.

Sacrette nodded at the dark figure, then said icily, "Good evening, Major Zuberov."

11

MAJOR SERGEI ZUBEROV WAS WAITING IN THE PAS-
sageway outside the operations center of the *Novorosiysk*.
He paced nervously, smoking heavily on a cigarette.

He didn't want to be on this mission any more than
Sacrette. He was needed elsewhere. In Azerbaijan where
trouble was brewing. Where his father commanded the
southern defense forces of the Soviet air defenses.

The sound of clicking heels brought him to attention
when Galenin approached.

Stopping beside the young aviator, the Admiral shot
Zuberov a warning glance. Then removed all doubt about
his expectations.

"I know these are difficult times for you, Sergei.
Your father is a close friend of mine. But we have our
duty. You must not let your personal problems interfere.
Not the problems with Sacrette, nor the situation with
your father. Is that perfectly clear?"

Zuberov nodded weakly. "Has there been any word
since I left the air base at Baku?"

Galenin shook his head sympathetically. Motioning
to the door, he said softly, "Come. We have a difficult
task. One that must succeed."

Galenin entered first, followed by Zuberov.

Sacrette was standing off to himself. When Zuberov appeared his fists tightened.

Were it not for the mission, he might well have ended the feud then and there.

But, he thought to himself, *there will come another time*.

The glaring Zuberov seemed to be thinking the same thought.

12

2155.

Captain Shoukry Khattree lay expectantly in the center of a round bed he found intriguing, and somewhat surprising. The bed rotated in a full circle every five minutes.

He felt lightheaded. Giddy. Was it the forbidden wine? Or the even more forbidden hashish?

Or the excitement of the woman slowly undressing beyond the nylon veil enveloping the circular bed?

She was, he knew, the most forbidden of all.

Looking up, he saw his nude body reflecting off the mirrors covering the ceiling above the bed. His body was young, powerful. His member rose from his groin like a giant lance ready to thrust.

His excitement intensified as the curtain separated and the woman knelt on the side of the bed. She smelled of the incense filling the room; her eyes were wide, oval, vacant from the hashish.

Slowly, she crawled toward him, inching her way like a tiger stalking her prey.

Shoukry quivered as her finger ran a long, slow trail along his leg, to his groin, causing his stomach muscles to contract.

He wanted to praise Allah for his fortune, but could say nothing as she took control of his mind and body.

"You are so beautiful," he told her as he touched her breasts. The feel of her skin made him harden even more until he thought he would explode.

Teasingly, she removed his hand, then carefully guided her body on top of him, pinning him beneath her thighs. Powerful thighs. Surprisingly powerful, he thought.

Her lips touched his ear, nibbling the lobes in a slow, methodical rhythm.

"I must have you," he said, trying to rise. But she held him firmly against the silk sheets. Against his skin, the wetness of her vagina was accented by the absence of hair. She was shaved smooth.

"Now," he begged. "Now."

Reaching beneath her, she took his member and slowly stroked the shaft until his body began to move with the motion of her caress. Gradually, she lowered herself until he felt himself begin to glide into her wetness.

Staring at the mirrors, he could see her back twisting and turning above him.

He saw her hands rise to her head, where she removed something long and thin from her hair.

The coils of hair fell like heavy braided rope onto his face. The weight of her hair was surprising, as was the churning desire of her body.

He found himself being pulled deeper into her as her breathing became heavier. With each rise and fall of her body he was growing weaker.

Moments later he felt himself explode in a long, pulsating orgasm that seemed to drain him of his final strength.

Exciting. Exhausting.

Then painful.

A sharp sting knifed through his head. His ears began ringing as the room started to swirl. He tried to rise but was frozen as the muscles in his body refused to respond.

His eyes widened; there was a mixture of warmth and pain in his left ear. The ringing rose to a howl.

Mounted above him she began to laugh as he tried harder to move but felt nothing. Nothing.

Except the pain. And the draining of his strength.

Then, off the mirrors overhead, he saw, and understood.

She smiled down at him. The warmth seemed to flood from his ear as his body grew cold. So cold.

Seconds later, Shoukry Khattree was totally paralyzed. He felt his heart begin to fade and just before his central nervous system shut down, stopping his heart, he saw the instrument she had removed from her hair.

Only now the long pearl-tipped hairpin was incredibly shorter. Made shorter by the visible absence of the four inches of hairpin steel he knew had been shoved through his ear and was destroying his brain.

Only the pearl-tip was visible.

The instrument of his death was the last sight he saw before slipping into internal darkness.

That, and the incredible glow of triumph filling her face.

13

2200.

A LONG TABLE COMMANDED THE OPERATIONS CENTER of the *Novorosiysk*; computerized maps glowed from three walls surrounding the table. Sacrette couldn't help but notice the similarities in the Soviet interior design to that of the USS *Valiant*'s CIC.

He wondered if the layout had been stolen from the Americans. Probably, he thought sarcastically, staring across the table at Zuberov.

Two Americans were waiting when Sacrette arrived aboard the Soviet carrier. Both men sat on each side of the CAG; their discomfort was obvious as Sacrette and Zuberov stared hatefully at each other.

Sitting on Sacrette's left, Colonel John Baldwin, a retired air force fighter pilot, was studying reconnaissance photographs of the Iraqi complex at Al-Nasra. The military attache to the U.S. Ambassador to Jordan, Colonel Baldwin was an expert on Iraqi air operations, and the only black man aboard the Soviet carrier.

Elliot Smithson sat on Sacrette's right. He was the president's representative from the National Security Council.

"Gentlemen," Galenin began. "We are not here to

debate the subject of Iraqi missile development. Or the threat such a capability may or may not pose to the balance of power in the Middle East. We are here to devise a military contingency plan should the political leaders of our governments decide a military option is required against the missile complex at Al-Nasra."

Galenin bowed slightly to Baldwin. "Colonel Baldwin will brief us on the current state of Iraqi military air defenses."

Baldwin began with a brief history. "Since we are primarily concerned with Iraqi defense forces, I will limit my comments to the interceptor and surface-to-air missile capability. In 1980, the Iraqis and Iran went to war, a war of attrition that inflicted heavy losses to the Iraqi air force. Losses which are being slowly replaced by a variety of countries, thus diluting the predominant Soviet content of the air force."

Baldwin paused to allow his words to have effect on the Soviets sitting across from him.

"Currently, the air defense is composed of approximately 10 MiG-25 'Foxbats,' 15 MiG-23 'Floggers,' and nearly 130 MiG-21 'Fishbeds.' Most of these squadrons are detailed along the Iranian border. Supporting the interceptors are several squadrons of Soviet-built SA-2, SA-3, and SA-6 surface-to-air-missile complexes. Again, most of these elements are assigned to protect Iraq along the Iranian border. However, there is one missile squadron deployed at Al-Nasra."

Admiral Galenin glanced to his left, to a Soviet officer wearing a uniform sparkling with decorations. "General Popov. What is the current status of the missile complexes?"

Yevgeni Popov, a major general in the Soviet air

force, was sitting next to Zuberov. As deputy commander of the southern region Theater of Military Operations of the *Voyska Protivovozdushnoy Oborony*—Troops of the Air Defense—he added a vital comment. "The Iraqi SAM complexes are presently operating at less than fifty percent launch capability due to delays in replacement." He grinned, then added wryly to Baldwin, "Much like the Iranians, who are unable to get replacement parts for their American-built equipment."

"What about Al-Nasra?" asked Sacrette.

Popov studied the CAG momentarily, as though suggesting he was possibly giving something away to the enemy. Then he shrugged. "SAM-2s."

"Mobile or entrenched?" asked Baldwin.

Popov motioned to a technician sitting at the end of the table. An overhead projector suddenly displayed the missile complex. Popov went to the screen, and with a pointer touched a dozen missile bunkers circling the complex. "The missiles are launched from entrenched positions."

Sacrette looked across the table at Zuberov. "Good. They'll be easy to knock out."

Zuberov nodded.

For the first time since meeting, the two men smiled at each other.

"The missile bunkers should pose no difficulty," agreed Popov. "However, the launch complex itself will be more difficult to destroy."

Popov pointed at the complex. Actually, he was pointing at a cropping of mountains rising from the desert floor.

"The research center is literally built underground."

Sacrette leaned forward, studying the display. He

could see the missile complex was built inside one of the mountains forming a tall, rocky fortress. His first thoughts flashed to another complex similar in design. The U.S. NORAD command center at Cheyenne Mountain, Colorado.

Then he realized what no one appeared ready to say.

"It'll take a nuclear warhead to destroy that complex."

14

"NUCLEAR WEAPONS ARE DEFINITELY OUT, CAPTAIN Sacrette." Baldwin was thumping a pencil nervously against a reconnaissance photograph.

Sacrette released a long sigh. The complex appeared impregnable. "I don't see any other way."

Smithson motioned to the others sitting at the table. "That's what we're here to determine. Another way. The United States and the Soviet Union cannot launch a nuclear strike against the complex. The political fall-out would be devastating. For the first time in forty years the world may be moving toward a peaceful coexistence. Jesus Christ! It would be a royal kick in the ass if the first U.S./Soviet joint effort was a nuclear strike against a third world country."

"What do you suggest?" asked Sacrette.

Smithson opened his briefcase and spread a map of the Al-Nasra area on the table. "There are three primary considerations to the strike: Iraqi air defenses, Iraqi ground forces at the airfield, and the research facility. The Soviet air force will provide fighter cover against Iraqi interceptors and attack craft. Soviet Naval Infantry airborne troops and U.S. Marine helicopter assault troops will deploy to take and secure the airfield and missile

---

installation guarding the complex. Once the airfield is secured the ground forces will establish a perimeter and await further instructions. We expect the Iraqis will pour some of their troops into the region once the balloon goes up. If so, the airborne and Marine troops can be used."

"What about the research and launch facility inside the mountain?" asked Sacrette.

Popov answered the question. "A combined force of Soviet Special Forces *spetsnaz* and Navy SEALs will penetrate the complex and destroy the research center with demolitions."

"What about the extract?"

Popov pointed to an airfield less than two miles from the base of the mountain. "The Marines will helo in and out in their aircraft under U.S. fighter TAC CAP. Soviet Antonov AN-124 Ruslan transports will land at the airfield and extract the Soviet troops."

There was still one question Sacrette needed answered. "What are the responsibilities of the carrier-based aircraft other than TAC CAP?"

"The responsibility of your air wing, Captain Sacrette, will be to provide TAC CAP cover during the operation, and destroy the SAM missile bunkers, the military barracks and aircraft at the airfield prior to the airborne and helicopter assault." Popov touched his pointer to a highway winding to the airfield. "Additionally, there is only one highway leading to the facility from Baghdad. Should troops be ferried into the action, your aircraft will prevent the Iraqi army from reaching the airfield or research complex by road."

"What about helicopters? Gunships and troop transports?" asked Sacrette.

Popov nodded to Zuberov. "Major Zuberov's MiGs

will intercept any helicopters dispatched to the fighting. Also, you will have aircraft flying a TAC CAP should anything get past Major Zuberov."

Baldwin jumped in with another suggestion. "We can throw a squadron of F-14 Tomcats into the fray to back up the Soviet interceptors. A squadron from the USS *Valiant*."

Sacrette released a long, low whistle. Shaking his head, he said what everybody was thinking. "We'll be declaring total war against the Iraqis."

Smithson spoke up. "What we'll be doing, Captain Sacrette, is sending a message to every country in the world who thinks they can upset the balance of power in any region through the use of nuclear weapons. A severe message. In the future, the U.S. and Soviet Union are going to clean up this world. Together. It's what the president and General-Secretary have agreed upon. All you have to do is look at the events of the past few weeks to see our nations are serious about bringing the world back from the brink of destruction."

Sacrette had to agree it was a good idea. Eastern Europe was changing with every tick of the clock. Communism, per se, was becoming a political suit of empty armor. The Warsaw Pact now stood in factions concerned with the internal problems of their respective countries. Talk was circulating that NATO would be disbanded in the future.

Peace, not war, between the U.S. and Soviet Union was a vision on the horizon.

A blurry vision; but a vision nonetheless.

"What about Arab intervention? From adjoining countries who are members of the Arab League?" asked Sacrette.

Smithson grumped. "Hell, they're the ones who stand to lose the most if the Iraqis develop long-range nuclear weapons. Especially the Iranians. They'll keep their mouths shut and their hands in their pockets."

Sacrette sat back. The plan was feasible. But it could be costly.

"It's possible," Galenin said hopefully, "that the Iraqis are not as advanced as our intelligence agencies predict. If that's the case, the military option will not be necessary."

Smithson shook his head. "That's doubtful. Our information appears reliable."

Nothing more was said. The men sitting at the table were all looking at the computer map depicting the missile research center at Al-Nasra.

All except two of the men. The two who would be in the thick of the fighting if the operation was mounted.

Sacrette and Zuberov were staring at each other. A strange, almost eerie light seemed to radiate from their eyes.

A shining light. The shining light of men who knew instinctively they were going into battle.

15

1000.

THE MOMENT THE USS *VALIANT* APPEARED ON THE horizon, an excitement theretofore unknown to Kuwait Bay began rippling through the ancient harbor. Hundreds of dhows set sail from the port that rested in the shadow of the brownstone Al-Seif Palace, the royal residence of the emir of Kuwait.

Hundreds of curious Kuwaitees began flooding the pier, pushing and shoving to view the giant warfaring complex that was making its first visit to their shores. Overhead, the sky drummed with the rotor slap of television news crews filming the carrier's entrance into the harbor.

The excitement was electric.

High above the crowd, from his position at the east wall of the Palace, Nemat Masud gazed through a pair of binoculars, watching intently as the island superstructure of the *Valiant* began to grow in size with the carrier's approach. Rising above him, a giant tower with massive clocks on all four sides stretched into the clear sky, a beacon to ships entering the harbor. Crowning the tower was a domed minaret plated in solid gold.

Soldiers patrolled methodically along the wall;

dressed in traditional Arab dress and wearing red kaffi-
yehs, the mark of the royal guard. They seemed to ignore
the approaching aircraft carrier.

They did not ignore Masud, the chief of the emir's
security force, whose dark features were sullen within
the framework of his thick beard.

Masud ignored the guards, and the crowd. All his
concentration was directed to the deck of the carrier.

"Splendid," he whispered aloud.

Crowding the flight deck was the full complement of
the Carrier Air Wing. Ninety-five aircraft of various types
sat parked tightly; the morning sunlight sparkled off the
freshly-polished metal.

"The helicopter is ready," a deep voice crackled
over the walkie-talkie dangling from his shoulder.

Masud turned to the west wall, where an Aerospatiale SA.330 Puma sat on the roof of the palace. Slowly,
the rotors began turning until the beat was steady.

Masud hurried to the Puma, running head down,
his robe flapping as the rotor wash swirled in the rising
heat. Entering the helicopter, he buckled himself into a
webbed seat.

A quick look of anger filled his face as he noticed
someone was missing. He spoke angrily to the royal air
force pilot. "Where is Yasmin?"

The pilot said nothing. Instead, he raised his hand,
pointing to a woman who was approaching along the
rooftop. She was tall and beautiful; she walked, rather
than hurried, further angering Masud.

Opening the door, Masud snapped at the woman.
"Hurry. We are late."

Yasmin Alabasi stepped elegantly into the helicopter. She ignored Masud's rebuke and motioned to the
pilot.

The Puma lifted off, then turned east toward the sea.

Over the roar of the engines Masud covered the final details of their assignment.

"The emir will officially greet the Admiral at the residence of the American Ambassador."

"How many officers will be in the Admiral's party?" she asked.

Masud took a folded piece of paper from inside his robe. "The Admiral and his aide. The remaining Captains of the American Battle Group will arrive later in the afternoon at the official dinner party. But initially, the meeting between the emir and the Admiral is to be private."

She glanced at the helmeted head of the pilot and nodded approvingly.

As the helicopter neared the carrier, Yasmin took a small compact kit from her purse. Carefully, she examined her makeup. Satisfied that her face was flawless, she held the mirror to the most prominent feature on her head.

Her long black hair lay in heavy braids coiled on her head. Holding the braids in place was a pearl-tipped needle.

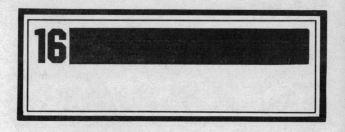

16

"IT'S ABOUT DAMNED TIME," SAID LIEUTENANT JEFF-rey 'Bone' Armitage. The young officer's face frowned beneath high, protruding forehead bones, which had automatically spawned his running name in flight school.

Admiral Lord was standing on the flight deck dressed in his white uniform, as was his aide, Lieutenant Armitage, who was unable to hide his displeasure with the late-arriving representative from the emir of Kuwait.

Lord didn't appear ruffled by the tardiness; unlike his new aide, he knew diplomatic protocol was not always dependable whether the guest was an admiral or a president.

Standing behind Admiral Lord was Captain Freeman Purcell, the newly-assigned executive officer of the *Valiant.* He would be in command of the carrier, as well as the Battle Group during Lord's visit to shore. A seasoned veteran of Vietnam, and the invasion of Grenada, Purcell was the exact opposite of Admiral Lord.

Short, barrel-chested, and often gruff to the point of being rude, Purcell was disliked by the men and officers of the *Valiant.* In the two weeks he had shipped aboard he had managed to incur the anger of everyone he met, with the exception of Lord, with whom he had graduated at Annapolis.

"He won't win any popularity contests," Lord had told Sacrette when the new exec and the CAG locked horns over flight operations. "But he's a good man in a shooting war. He's tough as nails. And fearless."

Standing behind Purcell was CPO Farnsworth, whose face streamed with sweat from the heat. As the emir's private helicopter landed, Farnsworth and three enlisted men marched briskly to the Puma.

"Welcome aboard the USS *Valiant*." Farnsworth saluted as Masud popped through the door.

The chief then stepped aside as Admiral Lord and Armitage approached.

Masud apologized, then invited Lord into the helo. Armitage followed, and within seconds the giant Aerospatiale was lifting off the flight deck.

Settling into the webbed seat beside Masud, Lord told the emir's security chief, "I could have flown to the meeting aboard one of my helos. I brought several along." He grinned proudly as he nodded at the flight deck; a variety of helos were lined up in neat rows below it.

Masud smiled diplomatically. "The emir is a man who prides himself on protocol, Admiral. In Kuwait, we try to meet all the needs of honored guests."

Lord started to respond when he felt the sudden change of the helicopter's flight attitude. The helo was in a steep angle of attack, diving toward the surface of the sea.

"What the hell?" Armitage shifted toward the admiral but was frozen by the appearance of the unexpected.

Masud's eyes widened on the right hand of Yasmin Alabasi.

She was gripping an automatic pistol.

"Are you insane?" shouted Masud.

"Keep quiet and do as you're told and you will not be harmed," she snapped at the security chief.

There was the sensation of the helicopter banking sharply. Through the cockpit window Masud saw the coast of Kuwait begin to fade as the helo turned toward the northeast.

It was then he realized what was happening. Sitting in the front seat, the pilot had removed his helmet.

"Where is Shoukry?" Masud demanded of Yasmin, but he was glaring at the pilot. A man he had never seen before.

"He's dead." Yasmin replied calmly.

Bone Armitage didn't know who they were talking about, and couldn't care less. He knew what was happening, and knew his duty. Without a word, he lunged for the woman holding the pistol.

He died the next instant. Yasmin fired one bullet, striking the young officer in the forehead. His body twisted sideways, then fell across Lord's knee, spewing bluish brains and red blood onto the admiral's white dress trousers.

In the ensuing confusion, Masud reached beneath his robe. His fingers were closing around the butt of a pistol resting in his shoulder holster when Yasmin's finger closed around the trigger of her pistol.

A short, crisp bark of the pistol registered the end of Nemat Masud's life. His body pitched backward, still strapped to the webbed seat. His dead eyes stared emptily beneath a bullet hole in his forehead.

Yasmin trained the pistol on Admiral Lord, who still sat pinned beneath the dead weight of Armitage.

"Sit very still, Admiral. As you can see I am very proficient at using this pistol."

Lord said nothing. His hands gently gripped the shoulders of his dead aide.

In the distance, a large river came into view. The river Euphrates emptied into the Gulf, a clear, tributary boundary.

To the west lay Iraq.

Judging by the flight of the Aerospatiale, their apparent destination lay to the east: a nation that considered itself at war with the United States.

Iran.

17

IN THE *VALIANT'S* CIC, THE RADAR OPERATOR SAW the emir's helicopter target disappear from the screen before any of the personnel on the flight deck knew what had happened.

"Holy shit. The admiral's helo has gone down!"

Charging out of his chair, the tactical air officer was at the screen in a heartbeat. In the next heartbeat he was talking over the 5-MC loudspeaker.

"Launch search and rescue. Repeat. Launch search and rescue. The admiral's helo is down." The TAO's voice boomed over the flight deck.

Farnsworth ran furiously to the starboard side of the flight deck. In the distance he could see the image of the Aerospatiale growing smaller as the helo raced to the northeast.

"Kiss my fucking ass." Farnsworth cursed as he realized the helicopter had not gone into the water.

Purcell came charging to the chief's side in time to see the helo disappear at the horizon. "What's happening?"

Diamonds pointed toward the horizon. "The helo hasn't gone in the drink, sir. But it's sure as hell gone. Toward Iran!"

"Christ," Purcell spit out, running toward a "bat phone," one of the telephone stations linked to critical personnel on the carrier. "Launch the Alert Five. Launch the Alert Five."

Seconds later the voice of the air boss boomed through the confusion on the flight deck. "Launch the Alert Five. Launch the Alert Five."

Lt. j.g. Ryan "Rhino" Michaels closed the canopy of his F/A-18 Hornet and ran the power to full military. His eyes were locked on the bow catapult officer who sat at his control console between the waist and bow catapults.

At the console, the BCO glanced at the bow safety officer, who was kneeling beside the Hornet with his left thumb extended into the air, signaling that the Hornet was ready for launch.

Glancing at the signal lights on the island, the BCO saw the lights turn from yellow to green. He smartly saluted Rhino, who returned the salute and sat back hard into his ejection seat.

The moment the BCO pressed the firing button, the huge steam-driven pistons beneath the flight deck shot forward, hurtling the Hornet into the air like a bolt from a crossbow.

Two seconds later the Hornet was off the deck, with Rhino taking the throttles past military power into Zone Five afterburner. When the roar hit the air above the flight deck, the Hornet was already banking toward the northeast in pursuit of the helo.

"We gotta hustle or he'll be long gone to Ragland," shouted Rhino's RIO Lt. j.g, Sean "Gooze" Thomas.

Rhino shoved the nose forward, riding a carpet of pure afterburner as fuel was injected directly into the flames at the engine's exhaust nozzles.

Seconds later, the Hornet went through Mach one in pursuit of the helicopter.

"Got him on radar," Gooze looked at his radar scope. The single blip on the screen was flying a straight path. "He'd not flying evasive."

"Why should he?" countered Rhino as he saw the coast of Iran coming closer. "The bastard's holding all the aces."

Gooze looked up from the console. "Let's scope him out."

Approaching the Puma, Rhino eased back on the power, slowing the Hornet. He dropped flaps, then landing gear, bringing the Strike/Fighter to 160 miles-per-hour, the flat-out speed of the Puma.

The Puma was off their port wingtip when Rhino glanced at the helo. What he saw made his blood chill.

"Christ!" Rhino breathed into his mask.

"Those sons of bitches!" Gooze replied, staring at the opened door of the Puma.

Admiral Elrod Lord was kneeling in the open door. Behind him stood a woman holding a gun to the admiral's head.

Cradled between Lord's legs was a young officer dressed in a white naval uniform, his tunic soaked with blood.

There was a hush, then Rhino reported to the carrier. "Wolf Five to Home Plate . . . have helo in visual. Admiral alive but captured. Bone appears to be dead."

An uneasy pause followed, then the voice of Purcell ordered, "You're approaching Iranian air space, Wolf Five. . . . Break off contact. Return to carrier."

Reluctantly, Rhino cleaned up the flaps and gear,

then lit the afterburner, just as the plane was entering Iranian airspace.

As the Hornet banked sharply, they saw a sickening sight that put their sense of discipline to the ultimate test.

A sickening ache kicked at their stomachs as they saw something fall from the Puma.

In the CIC, Purcell heard the nearly imperceptible voice of Rhino report.

"The bastards just dropped the Bone into the ocean."

18

CAG SACRETTE BEGAN MONITORING THE COMMUNI-
cation between Wolf Five and the CIC from forty miles
east of Al-Kuwait. His stomach was in knots when he
heard the admiral's aide had been thrown into the sea.

It was that single act of human disregard that over-
powered his military discipline to the point where he
knew what had to be done.

Dropping to the deck, Sacrette flew the Harrier on
an intercept course that carried him over the southern
tip of Iraq, across the Euphrates, into Iran.

Flying twenty feet above the ground at 700 miles-
per-hour, he caught up with the Puma sixty miles inside
Iran.

Switching to satellite communication, he contacted
the carrier, reporting, "This is Wolf One . . . have Puma
in sight. Switching to television cameras for real-time
transmission."

In the CIC, the image of the Puma was transmitted
onto one of the television screens lining the wall. The
image of the Puma came in clear.

"Be advised, Captain Sacrette, you have penetrated
foreign air space. You are ordered to return to the carrier
at once. Do you understand?" Purcell's voice was laced
with acid.

"Get this television transmission into the threat library, Captain Purcell. At the same time get this thought into your head . . . I'm not leaving until I know where they're taking Admiral Lord. Wolf One . . . out."

Sacrette hit the cold switch on his radio, terminating communications with the carrier.

Five minutes later the Puma banked northwest, toward the Iraqi border. The terrain was rugged, desolate, devoid of all life, human or otherwise.

Sacrette dogged the trail until the blip on his radar screen became stationary. At that point he was faced with a decision: to proceed, and risk discovery, letting the kidnappers know their location was compromised; or, to return to the carrier and plug the coordinates into satellite surveillance.

The decision was a difficult one. He made it reluctantly. Turning back toward the sea, he took a map from the lower pocket of his speed jeans. A careful study of the map revealed only one name marked in the general area. A small village he recalled hearing about when he was assigned during the 70s as an F-14 Tomcat flight instructor with the Shah of Iran's air force.

The small village of Kims. For all intents and purposes totally useless, except for its historical legend.

There was a monastery in Kims founded in 1096 by a fanatical group sworn to protect the sacredness of the Koran, and punish infidels judged to be enemies of Islam.

These were the followers of Hassan ibn al-Sabbah, known to his enemy as "The Old Man of the Mountain."

His followers were called the *Hashishi*.

Holy assassin.

The *Hashishi* was destroyed after the Crusades, but legend had passed down that the *Hashishi* had secretly resurfaced through a small group of descendants of the original "Old Man of the Mountain" and his successors, who were also called "The Old Man of the Mountain." Each was a mullah sworn to protect and avenge their sacred land.

The cult was not called the *Hashishi*; they gave themselves a name more indicative of their modern purpose.

They called themselves "The Guardian of the Koran."

The *Hafiza*!

PART THREE: ██████ THE DUNGEONS OF KIMS

19

Captain Purcell was leaning against the coaming of the bridge, staring hatefully at the flight deck below. He was tired, angry, and knew his tail section was hanging in the fire. The fact that he was being questioned again, by the same person, merely increased his annoyance.

"The Iranians are not only disavowing any responsibility for the kidnapping of Admiral Lord, they are taking it one step further by insisting that if there was a kidnapping, it was the work of the Iraqis."

"That's bullshit!" snapped Sacrette. The CAG was nose-to-nose with the *Valiant*'s executive officer. His eyes were hooded, giving him the look of a cobra ready to strike. "You know damn well it was the Iranians. Question is: What are you prepared to do?"

"Nothing," Purcell retorted.

"Nothing!" Sacrette's fists were balled; his look was incredulous.

"That's correct, Captain. Nothing. I'm going to do nothing until I get orders from the Pentagon. Meanwhile, I suggest you put the wraps on that French-Canadian temper of yours and conduct yourself like an officer in the United States Navy. Which means, keep your mouth shut, your hands in your pockets, and stay the hell out of the way. This is now a diplomatic problem. It'll be resolved by diplomats."

"Diplomatic my ass. That's my commanding officer those bastards grabbed. A man I served under through Vietnam, Grenada, and half-a-dozen more shooting matches. He wouldn't leave me to the diplomats. Nor you, for that matter."

Purcell clasped his hands behind his back and released a long, heavy sigh. He was trying to ignore Sacrette. Enough had been said as far as he was concerned. Further argument could only lead to charges of insubordination. He turned to a sailor standing by the captain's chair on the starboard side of the bridge.

"Chief Farnsworth, I want you to escort Captain Sacrette to his quarters. He is to remain there until further orders. Is that clear?"

Farnsworth looked like a man ready to eat fire. When he said nothing Purcell's voice barked sharply.

"Goddammit, Chief. Is that clear!"

Farnsworth jerked to attention. He was trapped in an enlisted man's worst nightmare: caught between two arguing captains. "Yes, sir." He looked at Sacrette, nodding his head toward the door. "You heard the captain, Thunderbolt."

Sacrette turned to leave when a communications officer entered the bridge. "Telephone call, sir. From the U.S. ambassador to Kuwait, Ambassador Sheffield."

Purcell held up his hand to Sacrette, halting his departure. He took the telephone from the console and spoke for several minutes. When finished, he turned to the CAG.

"That was Ambassador Sheffield. A preliminary investigation in Al-Kuwait has turned up a few answers. Not many but a few."

Sacrette relaxed slightly. "Do they know how the terrorists got their hands on the emir's helo?"

Purcell nodded. "The emir's pilot. A captain named Shoukry Khattree was found murdered an hour ago."

"Where did they find the body?"

"In the apartment of the emir's private secretary. Yasmin Alabasi."

"She must have been the woman reported in the helo."

"Yes," Purcell replied. "Facts are sketchy, but it appears she killed Captain Khattree—or had him killed—then replaced him with a double. It makes sense. She would have been able to get the phony pilot past palace security to the roof where the helo was parked."

"What about the security chief?"

Purcell shrugged. "They don't know anything. However, they suspect he was either an accomplice, or killed after lifting off from the *Valiant*. In either case, he's out of the picture."

"What about the woman? How could a woman get that close to the emir and be tied in with terrorists? Don't they run security checks?"

"They ran a thorough security check. She arrived in Kuwait five years ago. Attended the university. Graduated with high honors. She was personally selected by the emir."

" 'Arrived?' " Sacrette's voice was tinged with suspicion.

Purcell shook his head in disgust. "She was a refugee."

Before Purcell could continue, Sacrette held up his

hand. "Let me guess. She was a refugee from Iran. Right?"

"That's correct. It seems she developed influential contacts in the government while working her way up the ladder."

"You mean she fucked her way up the ladder."

"More than likely. She must have been working for the Iranians all along. Biding her time for the right moment when she would be the most useful."

There was no hiding the disgust Sacrette was feeling. He looked at Farnsworth. "Come on, Chief."

Sacrette stormed out of the bridge. Farnsworth followed close on his heels, watching the enraged CAG work his way through the bowels of the carrier like a wild bull.

In his quarters, Sacrette took a bottle of Jack Daniels from his clothing locker. He sat on his bunk and took a long pull from the whiskey, then handed the bottle to Farnsworth.

After the chief downed a healthy pull, Sacrette looked at him for a long moment. "Chief, I need a favor."

"Oh, shit. If you need a favor while under house arrest it can only mean one thing. In which case, I better have another bite of this snake venom."

Farnsworth downed half the bottle, then listened to the CAG's request. When Sacrette was finished, Farnsworth turned the Jack Daniels straight up to twelve o'clock and drank until his eyes were slightly glazed.

Five minutes later he slipped out of the CAG's quarters knowing Sacrette's request would cost him one of three things. All of which he owed to Sacrette.

His stripes. His career. Or his life.

20

ADMIRAL ELROD LORD WAS SITTING WITH HIS BACK against a stone wall; a rank, dusty smell permeated the room, which he knew was deep beneath the monastery where he was being held prisoner. The floor was dirt; hard, compacted dirt that had become like concrete since it had first been excavated in ancient time.

But the hardness of the floor wasn't the worst aspect of the situation; not by a long shot. The worst thing was the darkness.

The blackness enveloping the room was rich and velvety to the point where he thought he could see an image reflecting from his brain into his eyeballs.

The image of Lt. j.g. Armitage. Through the blackness he saw the white, bloodstained tunic. The dead, half-closed blue eyes.

The cold-blooded bitch with the smoking pistol. Then, her knee in his back, driving the limp body of his aide from his arms into the Persian Gulf.

How he hated her. Hatred like he had never known. Not in war. Never. A pure hatred. One that could never be satisfied.

Except possibly by . . .

The ring of metal against metal jerked him upright.

A move he regretted instantly as his skull cracked against something above his head.

Pain shot through his body, weakening his legs; legs he urged to move. To stand.

He didn't want to face his captors on his back.

Through the haze he saw a door opening. Light bled through the crack that slowly grew wider until the door was fully opened.

Suddenly, the flame of a lantern filled the opening. The lantern moved toward him, slowly, metronomically, swinging lightly from an extended arm.

"Who are you?" Lord demanded in a crisp military voice.

He could see a figure materialize as the light filled the room. Glancing quickly around, he saw a stark, barren room with no comforts. And the heavy ring embedded in the wall behind him.

He realized it was the ring he had struck when standing. The metal ring held a gnarled, rusted length of chain that glowed yellow with corrosion beneath the lantern light.

"Who are you?" Lord asked again. His voice was less severe as the figure stepped closer.

He could smell the breath of the lantern holder. Foul. Like decaying teeth.

The figure sat the lantern on the hard dirt floor, then sat cross-legged. When a voice spoke, it was harsh, like the howl of a desert wind. An old man's voice. "You will please sit."

Lord saw a bony hand flash past the light; a twisted finger pointed at the floor.

"You will please sit."

Lord seated himself in front of the lantern. The old

man moved closer until the admiral could see a face as ancient as the dungeon glowing from behind the light. From within a thick beard, his face was nearly hidden by a hood from his robe.

"I am Hakim," said the old man.

"Admiral Elrod Mathias Lord. United States Navy," Lord replied in smart military fashion.

"Yes. Admiral Lord. I have been waiting," said Hakim.

"Waiting?" Lord asked curiously.

"For many years. But that is a discussion we will have at another time. For now it is important that you know there is no escape. Not from this cell. Nor from our justice."

"Justice? You speak of justice. You who have murdered and kidnapped. What justice could you want from me?"

The old man leaned forward, adjusting his weight. In the light, Lord saw something swing from Hakim's neck. It was there for only a moment, then disappeared into the folds of his robe.

But he saw it. He had seen it before.

"That medallion. I have seen it before. In Malta. The circle of sevens."

Hakim's twisted fingers clutched the medallion, and as he leaned to the light, the metal glowed. As did his face. A face that seemed as old as the dungeon.

There was the slight suggestion of pain in Hakim's voice as he replied. "The medallion in Malta was worn by my nephew. He was killed by one of your men. For that, you shall pay, along with your other crimes."

"What crimes!" Lord was growing tired of the cat-and-mouse games.

"Crimes against my family. My country. My Allah."

"That's bullshit. Your nephew was killed while trying to attack foreign heads of state."

"For his failure he paid with his life. As you will pay with your life for his death and the death of others in my family."

Lord ignored the threat. There was something he still needed answered. Something that had begun that night in Malta. "Why did you attempt an attack against the president and General-Secretary?"

"It was a political matter. One you need not be concerned with."

"Whose politics? Iran's? That doesn't make sense. An attack against the United States president and Soviet General-Secretary would have brought severe repercussions against your government. Not even *your* government is that reckless."

Hakim laughed softly. "We have no government. We serve only Allah. And ourselves."

"Who are you?"

"We are the *Hafiza*. The Guardians of the Koran. The purifiers of Islam."

"What is your purpose?"

"To reclaim Persia."

Lord nodded. He was beginning to understand. "Azerbaijan."

Hakim bowed his head slightly. "You are very perceptive."

Lord knew recent riots by Muslims in the southern Soviet republic of Azerbaijan were putting a great deal of pressure on Soviet relations with Iran. Relations General-Secretary Gorbachev was trying to mend in order to prevent the fomenting of religious disturbances among the fifty-five million Azerbaijani Muslims.

"So you intend to stir up the Muslims, using revolt to destroy the relationships with the Soviets and Iranians."

"There will be jihad in Azerbaijan. Like the holy war in Afghanistan. The Russians will be forced to allow Iran and Azerbaijan to reunite. Then Persia will be reclaimed."

"You speak of a war the Tehran government couldn't possibly support, not since it got its tail shot off with the Iraqis. The government has depleted its military reserves, manpower, lost billions in oil production, and can't rebuild its war machine. The Iranian government couldn't finance a whorehouse, much less a holy war inside Azerbaijan."

Hakim laughed again. "As I said, it is a political matter. Not one of your concerns."

"Right. I should be concerned with justice. That was the word you used. Justice. For what reason?"

A deep sense of sadness filled the old man's face. He reached into his robe and withdrew a folder. Carefully, he spread the folder open. Thumbing through the pages he removed a newspaper clipping.

"For this. You are one of the infidels I hold responsible." Hakim handed Lord the clipping.

In the yellow light Lord examined the photograph in the clipping. He recognized the face of the man framed in the *Navy Time's* photograph. He remembered the caption:

CAG Sacrette claims first kill for USS Valiant!

Lord straightened. "Who are you?"

Hakim held his medallion to the light. His fingers touched the medallion lovingly. "I am the imam Hakim al-Sabbah Bakr. Head of the House of Bakr."

"Bakr?" Lord asked. The name sounded vaguely familiar.

Hakim nodded at the clipping. "Yes. Bakr. The father of Abdullaran Bakr. My oldest son. Father of the pilot killed by this man. One of your pilots!"

21

THE NAVY'S MOST INDISPENSABLE, AND PERHAPS POWerful, asset is the chief petty officer. It was with this knowledge that CPO Diamonds Farnsworth felt confident he could achieve most of what Sacrette had requested. Whether the full order would be filled would depend on Sacrette. Whom he wasn't certain of.

After all, Sacrette was a captain. Slipping through naval cracks wasn't accomplished by rank. It was accomplished through time-honored tradition.

One of the most honored traditions was that nobody fucked with a CPO.

Not even admirals.

Standing at the quarterdeck, he saluted the officer of the day and strutted toward a helo preparing for a hop into al-Kuwait to gyro back to the carrier with some dignitaries waiting at the embassy.

Sliding into the SH-60B Seahawk as though he owned it, he said nothing. A flash of his passport was enough authority. That and his rank. Minutes later the giant helicopter lifted off the flight deck and made the short ride to the American embassy.

After getting his passport stamped he went next door to the Kuwait Hilton where he caught a taxi. A hectic three-mile ride wound through the fashionable Bnaid Al-Ghar district, with its plush homes, to the business and shopping district of Fahed Al-Salim Street.

On Fahed, near the traffic ring, he found the street number of the shop matching the number on the paper given him by Sacrette.

It wasn't what he was expecting. Not for what he would be requesting.

The name of the business was in bold letters in both English and Arabic.

Mostafavi's Rare Books and Coins. International Dealers.

Inside, the shop smelled of fresh paint. Glass cases displayed rows of expensive coins. Gold Kruegerrands. Gold Dinars. A rare silver siglos from the reign of Croesus. A gold Byzantine solidus depicting Basil I and his son. And a rare 1874 American three-cent copper and nickel coin in mint condition.

And there were books, the most impressive being the complete leatherbound first edition of Alfred Lord Tennyson.

The place reeked of money. Big money.

"May I help you?"

Farnsworth turned to see a tall, dark, elegantly dressed man. The CPO smiled politely. "I'm looking for Mr. Mohammad Reza Mostafavi."

"I am Mostafavi."

There was something about the man that seemed to demand respect. Perhaps the eyes, the deep, black piercing eyes that seemed to stray from nothing. The stature, which was square-shouldered.

But mostly, it was the steel hook protruding from

the left sleeve of his expensively tailored sport coat.

Farnsworth knew instinctively that the man with the black-diamond eyes didn't pick up that piece of hardware in a crap game. He spoke and moved like a warrior.

And Farnsworth knew that Sacrette had picked the right man.

"I have an urgent request from a friend," Farnsworth said, reaching into his pocket.

Mostafavi said nothing. Rather, he nodded permissively, suggesting that Farnsworth continue.

"He said you would know him by this." Farnsworth held out his hand. In the palm was a pair of gold aviation wings. Wings of the Shah of Iran's Royal Air Force.

Mostafavi took the wings and turned them over. Quickly, he held the wings close to his eye.

"These were my wings. My initials are on the back. MRM. I gave them to a very dear friend. An American pilot."

"He gave them to me. To give to you. He's in trouble."

Mostafavi said nothing. He went straight to the front door, turned the lock, put out the CLOSED sign, and pulled down the blinds.

Motioning to the back room, he guided Farnsworth through a curtained doorway. In the back, he stopped in front of a heavy steel door secured by a computerized locking system. His fingers punched in the digital code and the door swung open. At the same time, a light came on as Farnsworth watched Mostafavi enter the room.

"Please. Come in. We can talk in private."

Farnsworth entered the secured room and was immediately blown away by what he saw.

Except for the armory aboard the USS *Valiant* he had never seen such an extensive quantity and array of weaponry.

Mostafavi was more than a dealer in rare books and coins.

He was obviously an international arms dealer.

22

2000.

Lt. Rhino Michaels was doing what most pilots aboard an aircraft carrier do when they're not flying or performing other duties. He was sitting in the cockpit of his F/A-18 Hornet, wearing his helmet. The visor was turned down, visibility blacked out by the Velcro protective cover that was attached to the visor when not in use, to prevent scratching.

The Hornet was parked on the hangar deck. It was quiet, except for the occasional sound of equipment being moved on the flight deck above. Personnel were gone. The lights were out except for red security lights and the white lights denoting auxiliary power boxes.

He was leaning back in the cockpit, his hands gripping the HOTAS. The safety switches on the ejection seat had been carefully examined prior to sitting, so he knew there was no fear of a premature ejection.

His thoughts were locked onto the HOTAS. Specifically, he was practicing, switching from one system to another while mentally engaged in air combat with a fictional opponent.

Like a piccolo player, his fingers moved about the control column, pressing whatever system he needed, whether fuel, communications, or weapons.

It was the way Strike/Fighter pilots kept their reflexes honed.

He was diving onto an opponent, then coming out of a steep turn, about to fire when he heard the sound of footsteps clicking across the metal floor.

Flipping the visor up, he saw a man walking through the hangar deck toward the stairs near elevator three.

The sailor was dressed in dungarees, blue shirt, and white Dixie cup hat. Not unusual for an aircraft carrier. Thousands of such enlisted men would be walking about.

What made him curious—rather, suspicious—was the swagger from the enlisted man.

And he knew immediately the man was not an enlisted man, but an officer and sometime gentleman.

Only one man in the world walked with that definitive, arrogant swagger.

Rhino quietly lifted himself out of the cockpit and followed the sailor, making certain to keep his distance.

Down the stairs and onto the fantail he followed.

On the fantail, the sailor was keeping to the shadows, being careful to avoid the officer on fantail watch.

"You sly son of a bitch," Rhino whispered aloud as he watched the sailor sneak down a ladder extending toward the water. There was only one place he could be going. And if so, only one thing he could do when he got there.

At the bottom of the ladder, the sailor paused, glanced around, then turned to the stern anchor cable.

Rhino blinked. And the sailor was gone.

Carefully, he sneaked to the edge of the fantail and peered down.

A grin etched his face. He wasn't sure what the sailor

was doing. But he knew there had to be a good reason.

He called softly to the figure ten feet below. "Good luck, Thunderbolt."

"Get the hell out of here," came a husky, low reply.

Rhino turned and walked away.

In the distance he could see the running lights of an approaching powerboat.

23

SACRETTE'S HANDS WERE NEARLY BLOOD RAW AS HE reached a point ten feet above the waterline. He wanted to say the hell with it and drop, but he knew that he might give himself away.

Painfully, he continued down, inching along the thick anchor chain until he felt his feet touch the warm water of Kuwait Bay.

Once in the water he began a long, steady swim toward a set of running lights a quarter-mile away. The swim was easy; refreshing. Allowing him time to think about what he was doing. More importantly, what he was going to do.

Nearing the boat, he heard a soft, familiar voice say, "How nice."

Sacrette laughed. It was the phrase he often used to politely tell someone to "kiss my ass."

At the bow of the powerboat, he looked up to see Farnsworth leaning over the side.

"What in hell are you doing here?" Sacrette snapped.

"Pulling your white ass out of the deep blue sea. And who knows, maybe a little later . . . out of the deep burning fire." The CPO extended his powerful hand to the CAG and pulled him aboard.

Before Sacrette could properly chew Farnsworth's tail section, another familiar voice called his name.

"Boulton. My friend." Mohammad Mostafavi stepped from behind the controls of the powerboat and came toward Sacrette.

The two men embraced like lost brothers.

"I knew I could count on you," Sacrette told the arms dealer.

"Y'all kiss. I'll drive." Farnsworth teased as he moved to the controls. In a matter of seconds the boat was cruising along the surface toward the openness of the Gulf.

Two nautical miles from the entrance to Kuwait Bay, Farnsworth eased back on the throttles to idle. He moved forward to where Sacrette and Mostafavi were drinking beer he had brought along.

"Pass me one. I might not get another one in this life," said Diamonds.

Beneath the radiant stars above the Gulf, the three men sat drinking beer. Farnsworth listened to the story of their friendship unfold.

"He was the best damn pilot in the Iranian air force, Chief. The best student I ever had, U.S. or Iran," Sacrette was beaming.

Mostafavi appeared embarrassed. "We had many good times, my friend. Many good times." Then a sadness came over his face.

Sacrette understood. He looked at Farnsworth, and explained a piece of Mohammad's life. "When the Ayatollah took over, Mohammad hung around for a couple of years. Until it got too crazy. Then one day, he lit the engine on his Tomcat, and hauled ass across the Gulf.

He spotted the carrier *Nimitz*, which was on tour of the Gulf Camel Station, and was granted permission to land."

Mohammad laughed. "Yes. It was a profitable morning."

Both men laughed. Farnsworth looked perplexed. "How?" he finally asked.

"You saw his business. It takes money to start a business. He sold the Tomcat to the U.S. Navy, moved to Kuwait, and became a wealthy businessman."

"No shit. You sold an Iranian F-14 Tomcat back to the United States?"

Sacrette clapped Mohammad on the back. "That's how he lost that hand. Arabs cut off the hand of a thief."

A silence followed. Then the two old friends laughed harder as Farnsworth appeared to believe the tale.

"No, Chief Farnsworth. I lost my hand a short while later. I used to cross the Gulf and smuggle Iranians out of the country. One night, we were attacked by a gunboat. I was shot in the hand." He made a cutting motion across the steel hook. "Now, I am not only considered a pirate . . . I look like a pirate."

Laughter echoed above the water, along with the cracking open of more beer.

When the beer, and the reminiscence was played out, Sacrette looked across the Gulf to where he figured the Euphrates lay. Tossing his empty bottle into the sea, he said flatly, "Gentlemen. Let's go get Admiral Lord."

Minutes later the powerboat was planed up at the bow, cruising effortlessly toward the northeast.

Toward Iran.

24

2115.

"GODDAMMIT. I SHOULD HAVE PUT HIM IN THE BRIG," Purcell stood trembling with anger.

The exec was standing in the red glow of the CIC. Four officers and eight enlisted sat frozen at their stations. All eyes were glued to a variety of radar screens. One of which was a satellite projection of the Gulf. On the northern tip of the Gulf a single radar blip was moving into Iranian territorial waters.

Commander Anthony Dominolli was standing at parade rest, his hands clasped behind his back. Perspiration was forming on his forehead and he wore the look of a man who definitely wished he were somewhere else.

Purcell looked at the blip, then back to Domino. "You know where he's going." It wasn't a question.

Domino's eyebrows rose slightly. "Yes, sir. I believe I do."

Purcell reached and touched the radar blip on the screen. After several seconds he went to another map displaying southern Iran. He studied the map for several minutes then turned to Domino. "You're to assume the duties of the CAG during Captain Sacrette's absence."

Domino snapped to attention and saluted. As he

was withdrawing from the CIC he noticed Purcell lift the red crypto telephone. He punched in several coded numbers.

Thirty miles away, the skipper of the troop transport USS *Minot* lifted his red telephone and heard the angry voice of the battle group exec order, "I want to speak with Lt. Colonel Henderson."

In his quarters belowdecks, Marine Lieutenant Colonel Walter Henderson was finishing his daily report when the telephone on his desk rang. He listened for several minutes, then considered the question Captain Purcell needed answered immediately.

"There's a lot of risk, but nothing my men can't handle, captain." Another question from Purcell followed. Henderson glanced at his watch, "I'll have one of my teams there in thirty minutes, sir."

Henderson hung up the phone and went to the quarters of one of his junior officers. He knocked, then stuck his head through the door.

Lieutenant Clay Dunstan was sitting on his bunk. He wore nothing but camouflage shorts, his powerful biceps rippling as he stood to attention.

Henderson stared approvingly at the young officer. Dunstan was short and powerfully built, his chest carrying the mark that identified him as one of the Marine Corps elite.

Two tiny scars marked the left side of his chest above the nipple. Scars he wore with pride.

When one of these elite Marines graduated from airborne school, a ceremony followed, inducting them officially into one of the finest military units in the world.

Stripped naked from the waist up, the graduates would place their newly earned gold airborne wings on their bare chests. The men they'd be serving with would pass by, one after another, welcoming the new member.

The welcome came in the form of a fist slammed against the wings. The two sharp pins meant to hold the wings to their uniform were driven into the flesh, leaving a mark that would stay with them forever. A mark to be worn with great pride.

Henderson proudly carried the same scar over his left breast. The mark of the "Eyes and Ears of the Corps." The mark of Marine Force Recon.

25

2230.

BUILT IN THE ELEVENTH CENTURY BY REMNANTS OF the *Hashishi*, the village of Kims had changed little in nine hundred years. The layout resembled a wheel, with the mosque positioned in the center. Streets ran from the mosque, appearing spoke-like; mud huts, bleached copper-white by the blistering sun, sat in rows along the streets. Two hundred in all; most were empty, filled only by the religious zealots who served the needs of the *Hafiza*.

Ancient. Unadorned. Except one.

Sitting on a hillock overlooking the village, the house of Bakr was as modern as the village was ancient. A six foot wall topped with broken glass and razor-sharp ribbon wire surrounded the house.

Over the main entrance, barred by a heavy wooden door was the sign of the House of Bakr.

A circle formed by the number seven.

Inside, flowers grew along the fringe of a lush green lawn concealing a maze of landmines and heat sensors. In the back, a swimming pool sparkled, reflecting the moon, which was full in the black sky.

Sabry Bakr walked naked from the house to the steps

leading into the turquoise water. His hard, muscled body gleamed from a fresh coat of ginseng oil.

Swimming to the center, he watched Yasmin Alabasi swim toward him. The sight of her nude body aroused him, as it always had since childhood.

"What about the Romanian?" Yasmin whispered.

Sabry shook his dark head. "Let him find his own woman."

They laughed. Then embraced. Legs twined. Mouths joined. Then his manhood found her lush gate.

They made love while turning in a slow circle, a gyration that increased in velocity as their passion heightened.

When Sabry reached orgasm, she exploded with him, churning the surface with her writhing. Her moaning lifted into the night, then drifted into an opened window at the side of the house.

Gheorghe Scornicesti lay on his sweat-soaked bed. The moaning of Yasmin cut like a knife. He had not been with a woman in three months, not since leaving Budapest and his mistress. Of her fate, and his wife, he knew nothing.

The fall of the Ceausescu regime had come suddenly, without warning.

All his plans now appeared lost with the revolution sweeping his homeland. Destroying his place of prominence. Destroying the Securitate.

Colonel Gheorghe Scornicesti had been the personal sword of the executed Romanian dictator, whose dead image he couldn't wipe from his mind. Ceausescu and his wife Elena. He had seen the dictator only one month earlier, on the doomed man's last trip to Tehran.

"It is very important that your mission remain a

secret. You cannot fail in this mission," Ceausescu had reminded him curtly in their secret meeting at the Romanian embassy.

Malta. He cursed the name. He cursed the inept Sabry Bakr, who was enjoying a beautiful woman while he languished in his sweat-stained bed.

He stood, convinced of his only chance of survival. Dressing quickly, he left his room and went to a room at the back of the house. Sabry Bakr and the woman were still in the swimming pool. The house was empty.

He opened a door that revealed a short flight of steps leading to a tunnel beneath the house.

Switching on a flashlight, he followed the tunnel running beneath the village.

As he walked, his heartbeat quickened. The eerie light shining off the tunnel walls reminded him of the maze of tunnels beneath the palace in Bucharest, where the loyal followers of Ceausescu had held out for days in their futile attempt to destroy the new government.

The tunnels had been their lifeline.

As this tunnel had now become the lifeline of Colonel Gheorghe Scornicesti.

Only he intended to survive!

26

ADMIRAL LORD RESTED ON THE TOPSIDE OF WHAT HE figured was his two-hundredth push-up. He had done two hundred sit-ups, and five hundred jumping jacks, as well as running in place for the entire chorus of the "Battle Hymn of the Republic," "Anchors Aweigh," and "The Two O'Clock Jump."

He was tired, but mentally fit. The most important tool for surviving captivity.

He had been fed once, a three-course meal consisting of bread, water, and a slimy soup he ate despite its grotesque taste.

He had been a prisoner in Korea before his escape in 1952. He knew the ground rules: Stay fit. Keep your mind active. And eat everything you're given no matter how god-awful the taste.

The isolation was the worst. Deprived of human contact, he fought the loneliness by reflecting on past memories, the good memories. Christmas with his wife and children. His first command as a carrier Battle Group commander.

Even his first kill over the skies of Korea.

What he refused to think about was the future. Tomorrow never comes for a POW. There is only the present.

"Come on, Fang. Get your ass moving," he called himself by his running name.

Down. Up. Down. Up. Twenty times. Then he paused. Not from fatigue, but because of a sound. A sound he recognized, but never expected to hear in the dungeons of Kim.

He crawled toward the sound, which was vague, distant. A tapping that seemed to beat through the darkness like his pulse.

Was it his pulse? he wondered. He stopped. Listening, he could hear his heart.

And the tapping.

"Christ," he said aloud, recognizing the sound.

He felt his way through the darkness until he touched the wall. The surface was smooth, slick like glass. Pressing his ear against the wall, he listened with an intensity he hadn't known except in aerial combat.

The taps came in sporadic bursts. Not very clear, but certainly identifiable.

The taps were short, followed by scrapes. He understood the use of the scrape. A long tap wouldn't transmit through the wall.

Only short taps. And scrapes for the long signal in the code.

Morse code, the pilot's international alphabet.

He listened and heard.

Tap. Scrape. Scrape. *W.*

Tap. Tap. Tap. Tap. *H.*

Scrape. Scrape. Scrape. *O.*

Who!

He didn't need to hear anymore. He knew the question.

Quickly, he took his flight wings from his tunic and began sending his message.

He tapped and scraped out the words, *American Pilot*. Then followed with the same question.

Who?

The taps and scrapes spelled out the identity of the person in the adjoining cell. What he heard was numbing. Confusing.

"How in the hell . . . ?" he asked the darkness.

Then he tapped and scraped another question. *How many?*

The reply said *four*, and asked *you?*

He signaled *one*.

When he asked *why?* The response was *ransom*.

The prisoners tapped out conversation until Lord had given the men in the adjoining cell his name, rank, and serial number.

The other prisoners did the same.

It wasn't until he mentally spelled out the last name of one captive that he said a word.

"My God." He started to send another signal when he heard the wooden bolt securing the cell door scrape.

He shoved his wings into his pocket and sat back.

The door opened slowly. The beam of a light filtered through, then struck his eyes, casing momentary blindness.

Holding his hand to his eyes, he saw a short, heavyset man standing in the doorway. The man was dressed in a uniform he hadn't expected to see in the Iranian desert.

Entering, he turned the light under his chin, revealing narrow features. His hair was blond. His eyes appeared blue.

"I am Colonel Gheorghe Scornicesti. Formerly of the Romanian army."

Lord stood. "I am Admiral Elrod Mathias Lord. Presently in the United States Navy. How can I help you?"

Scornicesti switched off the light. The sound of the door closing made Lord think the man had left.

He heard the man's heavy breathing, then his voice. "I have come to make you a bargain." .

Lord leaned against the wall. To Scornicesti he replied, "I'm listening."

27

UNLIKE ITS FOUR-LEGGED PREDECESSOR, THE MODern military "mule" thrives on gasoline, rather than hay. One similarity, however, remains—it was as uncomfortable as hell.

But just as efficient.

Sacrette was standing on the small, flat-surfaced "mule" Mohammad Mostafavi had brought from Kuwait City. The mule was easily transported aboard the powerboat, and once they had slipped through Iranian territorial waters to an isolated beach south of the village of Kims, the mule was unloaded.

Sacrette, Farnsworth, and Mostafavi were dressed in combat camouflage fatigues supplied by the arms dealer. They carried an array of weapons that included AK-47's, four LAWs rockets, a dozen grenades, an M-79 grenade launcher, and a SAW light machinegun.

They were dressed to the nines in fashions of death.

Sacrette figured they were within ten miles of the village. Scanning the desert night with starlight binoculars, he saw nothing threatening.

"Let's move out," he tapped Farnsworth on the shoulder. The CPO pressed the accelerator and the mule groaned forward on heavy tires designed for terrain negotiation, not smooth riding.

"Have you got any idea what the game plan is once we get to the village?" Farnsworth asked.

"Not the slightest. We'll reconnoiter, then lay out a plan."

"What makes you think they're still holding him in the village? He could have been moved to Tehran. Or a dozen other places."

Sacrette didn't think that was possible. "I thought about that possibility. But it's not likely. The helo went to the village. Not to Bandar Khomenyi, where there's an Iranian military base."

Farnsworth gave the reasoning some thought. "I see what you mean. If it was the Iranian government, they would have taken him somewhere secure, not to a monastery in the middle of the wilderness."

"Exactly. Which makes the situation that much more unpredictable."

"Why's that?" asked the CPO.

"We don't know who...or what we're dealing with."

"Terrorists?" Mostafavi asked.

"Yes. But what terrorists? If they're operating outside the Iranian government's knowledge, they'll be that much more dangerous."

"And cautious," added Farnsworth.

"I agree. I doubt we'll see flags flying when we get there." He paused, then turned to Mostafavi. "Do you know the story of the *Hashishi*?"

"The what?" asked Farnsworth.

"*Hashishi*," Mostafavi said. "An ancient cult of assassins organized in the eleventh century by a fanatical mullah, Hassan ibn al-Sabbah. In history, he was called

'The Old Man of the Mountain.' It was a cult of assassins who used hashish as part of their ceremonial preparation before seeking out specific targets. In those times, the targets were Turks. Later, it was soldiers in the Crusades. They reigned terror all over Persia. They believed they were specifically chosen by Allah to protect Islam, punish the infidel invaders, and seek His revenge. Anywhere in the world."

"Is it possible they have reemerged?" asked Sacrette.

"Why do you ask?" replied Mostafavi.

"I know the mosque at Kims was one of their monasteries. A training center for assassins. I learned that when I was stationed here in the seventies."

Mostafavi recalled the history of the country he could no longer live in. "Yes. Kims was one of many. There were hundreds at one time. After al-Sabbah died, a chain of mullahs took up the mantle of the 'Old Man of the Mountain.' It's possible they have been revived."

"What exactly was this cult?" Farnsworth asked Mostafavi.

"They were fanatical believers in the Koran. While the true assassins were called the '*Hashishi*,' and led by al-Sabbah, or his followers, they were guided by a council of elders. Mullahs. In the old days the council was composed of seven mullahs. They called themselves the '*Hafiza*.'"

"What does *Hafiza* mean?" asked Sacrette.

"The literal translation means 'guardians of the Koran.'"

Something Mostafavi said sparked a thought in Sacrette's mind.

"You said there were seven mullahs of the *Hafiza*?"

"That's correct."

"Did they have a sign? A symbol?"

"The symbol of the *Hafiza* was known only through the cult. But legend has it their symbol was in the shape of a circle. A circle of sevens. Which meant that any one of the seven mullahs was the leader. This protected the true 'Old Man of the Mountain' from being identified."

"And being assassinated," said Sacrette.

"You are right, Boulton. Even the Tehran government would fear such a cult. While Iran is considered a nation of religious fanatics, they do have their bounds of reason. Should the *Hafiza* resurface, the government knows it could become a target if it were judged by the purity of the Koran."

Sacrette remembered the medallion from Malta. Which suddenly made him recall something else; something that for years had been hazy, made unclear by the heat of battle. "I have seen that sign before, Mohammad."

"Where?"

"On two occasions. Two weeks ago in Malta, when we were assigned to protect the Summit At Sea. It was inscribed on a medallion worn by a terrorist who tried to create an international incident." Sacrette was careful not to reveal too much classified information.

"And the other time?" asked Farnsworth.

Sacrette shifted uncomfortably. He could see the F-14 Tomcat coming out of the turn in the skies high above the Persian Gulf. "In 1985. It was painted on the nose of a Tomcat I shot down."

Mostafavi recalled the incident. He had been in the Iranian air force at the time. "The pilot was a man I knew. His name was Abdullaran Bakr. A very mysterious man. And, yes, I recall he carried the sign of the *Hafiza* painted on his airplane. But he said it was only there to frighten Iraqi pilots who might engage him in combat. The way some of your pilots paint the skull and crossbones, or the Grim Reaper."

Mostafavi glanced at the fullness of the moon. "If it is true that the *Hafiza* has resurfaced and they do have Admiral Lord, then we must not fail."

"Why?" asked Farnsworth.

"The *Hashishi* were sent to assassinate. To instill terror. When an infidel was brought before the *Hafiza*, it was to stand in judgment. Judgment that had a prescribed punishment should the infidel be found guilty."

Sacrette didn't want to hear the answer, but he knew he had to ask. "What kind of prescribed punishment?"

Mostafavi's reply turned their blood to ice.

Sacrette pressed his foot down on the accelerator. "That's no way for any man to die."

28

"THAT'S AN INTERESTING PROPOSAL, COLONEL SCOR-nicesti. Certainly one worthy of consideration."

Scornicesti was standing by the door. The embers from his burning cigarette provided the only light in the cell.

"I doubt that you have any other option, Admiral. Your judgment will begin tomorrow. If you are found guilty—as I'm certain you will—your punishment will begin immediately. Do you know how they intend to punish you?"

"Firing squad. Drawn and quartered. I'm sure it'll be something memorable. I could taste the hate in that old bastard's soul. If he has a soul."

The cigarette twitched sideways through the dark-ness as Scornicesti's head shook. "No, Admiral. That would be swift for their tastes."

"Then tell me, damn you."

There was a pause, as though the Romanian was trying to enhance his position, his proposal. "Death by starvation."

Lord's stomach tightened. "Christ. That's bar-baric."

Scornicesti laughed. "You are dealing with barbar-ians."

"Something you seem to understand. You did say you were with the Securitate? Ceausescu's secret police. You and your men wore blue uniforms. Not the standard-issue brown uniforms."

"That is correct. I was in the Securitate. Now, I am a man without a country. Much like you. We can join together and live. Or stand alone and die. Slowly. Very slowly."

Lord didn't need to consider Scornicesti's proposal any further. It was the only chance he had in what he already knew was a deteriorating situation. "You have a deal."

The cigarette dropped to the floor. The admiral could see the man crush out the ash with his foot.

The darkness was complete.

As Scornicesti started to leave, Lord issued one final requirement through the darkness. "There's one more thing you have to do."

"Be careful, Admiral. You are not in a bargaining position. I'm a man of limited patience," the Romanian warned.

"You're a man whose balls are about to be hung in the fire."

"What do you want?"

"I want the men in the next cell. You know who they are. They're being held for ransom. They go with us."

Scornicesti's voice trembled through the darkness. "You are insane. Those men can barely walk. They have been here for three months. They will get us killed."

"We all go. Me. You. And the four hostages in the next cell. All or nothing. That's the bargain."

The door opened. The Romanian turned on his

flashlight. "Very well. We will take them with us."

Scornicesti made his way along the tunnel beneath the village. Once he reached the house, he switched off the flashlight and quietly climbed the stairs.

The door opened to something he wasn't expecting. A sweet fragrance filled his senses, flushing the stink of the dungeon from his mouth and nostrils.

He stiffened. There was the sound of movement. Against the moonlight spraying through the plate glass window of the front living room, he saw a shadow moving toward him.

"You were told to stay out of the tunnel, Colonel." The voice of Yasmin Alabasi drifted softly to him.

He heard the sound of a metal click. A sound he would recognize in a thunderstorm.

A light came on. She was standing in the alcove near the front door. In her hand she held an automatic pistol.

Scornicesti thought quickly. "The heat in this house is stifling. I was smothering. I went into the tunnel to cool my body." Then he went on the attack, the best defense. "The least you could do is air-condition this house. It is impolite to make a guest suffer such discomfort."

She was wearing a long, flowing nightgown. The curves of her body clung to the material where her skin, still wet from the pool, touched the fabric.

Her nipples gleamed through. Her hair was down, hanging in a long fall past her shoulders.

Yasmin's beauty was almost overwhelming. Scornicesti could have been easily aroused were it not for the gun. The sight of a woman gripping a pistol he knew she could use efficiently had the same effect on his loins as a bucket of ice water.

He bowed slightly. "My apologies for alarming you.

I will not go in the tunnel again, no matter how uncomfortable the heat."

As he started to leave, she cautioned him. "The next time you need to cool off... I suggest you take a swim. It's less dangerous."

Scornicesti returned to his room. He lay in a pool of sweat. His mind raced as he contemplated how he and the admiral would make their escape.

There was only one way.

He checked his watch.

0130.

He dared not sleep for fear he would not wake in time to set their plan in motion. Timing was of the essence.

Again he checked his watch.

0145.

Then he heard the howling.

29

SIROCCO!

The windstorm came out of the west, boiling across the desert beneath eighty-mile-an-hour winds. Particles of sand were suddenly as dangerous as bullets. Visibility was cut to zero. Not even the hands in front of their faces could be seen.

From their position overlooking the village, Sacrette, Farnsworth, and Mostafavi barely had time to crawl under the mule when the storm hit.

"Fuck," Farnsworth cursed beside Sacrette. "What are we going to do now, skipper?"

The CAG had seen siroccos before. The sandblast effect of the storm could strip paint from metal, flesh from bone. There would be nothing moving; neither man, machine, nor animal, until the storm blew through.

Which gave him an idea.

He turned to Mohammad. He pointed at the climbing rope draped around the arms dealer's shoulder. "Cut two lengths of rope. Make each length about five feet long."

That said, he took out his compass. Staring from beneath the mule at the curtain of sand swirling around them, Sacrette mentally envisioned the layout of the terrain surrounding the village. Terrain he had been examining through the night vision binoculars moments before the storm struck.

"What do you have in mind?" Farnsworth asked.

Sacrette grinned. "A crazy idea."

"Most of your ideas are crazy. But they always seem to work," Farnsworth replied. "Tell me what you've got in mind."

While Mohammad cut the climbing rope, Sacrette explained his plan to the men. The howl of the wind nearly drowned out his voice.

When Mostafavi was finished, the three men put on goggles Mostafavi had wisely brought along. Standing beside the mule, Sacrette tied an end of one length of rope to his webbed harness. The other end he tied to Farnsworth.

Farnsworth did the same, tying himself onto Mostafavi.

"A desert 'daisy chain,'" shouted Sacrette.

Taking the compass, he held the dial close to his face. Visibility was less than three inches, but it was enough for him to read the heading on the compass.

"The blind leading the blind," Farnsworth yelled.

Sacrette clapped the CPO on the shoulder, then shouted into his ear, "It's called taking advantage of opportunity, Chief."

Saying nothing more, the CAG started forward, feeling his way along the rugged terrain while keeping the compass needle pegged onto a distinct heading.

A heading that should lead him to a house on a nearby hill. The one he had seen through the night vision glasses.

The house bearing a sign on its front entrance.

A circle of sevens.

30

ONE LEVEL ABOVE THE DUNGEON, HAKIM AL-SABBAH Bakr lay on the reed mat in his cubicle, which was no more than a cell. The furnishings were spartan: there was a table, chair, and lantern for reading. Only one book lay on the table. The only book he needed to read.

The Koran.

He had been awakened by a strange sound. One he had never heard in his decades of living in the mosque. Rising, he dressed in his robe and hurried through the door.

The howling of the storm was reduced to nothing more than a low moan through the thick walls. Carrying a lantern, he walked down the steps leading to the dungeon.

Pausing at a heavy wooden door, he pricked up his ears. Listening.

The tapping was louder.

The wooden bolt creaked slightly as he opened the door. The light spilled into the room, framing Admiral Lord in the corner.

He held his gold aviator wings in his hand.

"Very ingenious, Admiral." Hakim motioned to the wall. "So you have discovered our other visitors."

Lord stood. "Why are they here?" he demanded.

Hakim smiled. "They will serve their purpose when the time comes."

"You're inhuman," Lord replied. "Keeping men locked away in dungeons. They told me they've been here for three months. They're sick. They need medical attention."

Hakim nodded. "Sick men are easier to manage. During their first days here they were a great deal of trouble. Now they are like sheep."

"You bastard." Lord started toward the old man.

Hakim's eyes narrowed. It was the first time Lord could recall the man showing emotion.

Emotion, and a pistol that materialized from beneath his robe.

"You are a very foolish man, Admiral." The pistol was leveled at Lord's chest.

Lord stood his ground. "Go ahead. Kill me. I prefer death from your pistol than from starvation."

Hakim's face hardened. Suspicion caused his eyes to flutter. "Why do you say that?"

Lord realized his mistake before the words had left his mouth. There was no backing away from the madman. He inched closer. "Isn't that the way you kill people? By starvation?"

"Who have you been talking to!" Hakim's voice shrilled through the dungeon. His eyes were two flames of hatred. Of suspicion.

"Go piss up a rope!" Lord said as he edged a step closer.

"Who!"

Lord lunged from three feet away. Nearing Hakim he heard the explosion, felt the crack against his skull.

The lantern in the old man's hand seemed to fly wildly about the room.

As he fell to the hard floor, nausea set the room to spinning.

Lord looked up to see the old man turn and leave the room. There was the sound of the wooden bolt closing.

The sound of the old man's feet padding hurriedly off the hardened floor.

And the darkness.

Then silence. And blackness as he slipped into unconsciousness.

31

COLONEL GHEORGHE SCORNICESTI HEARD THE ROAR of the pistol shot. He was halfway along the tunnel leading to the dungeon when the explosion turned him around, sending him hurrying frantically back toward the house.

Running for his life, he paused at the foot of the steps to catch his breath. From behind he could hear the sound of footsteps along the tunnel. Then a light appeared through the darkness. The dancing shadows preceding the light danced ghoulishly off the walls.

He had to escape.

Quietly, he slipped up the stairs. He had to reach his room.

"You were warned not to go in the tunnel!" The voice of Yasmin Alabasi cut through the darkness like a scalpel.

Scornicesti froze in his tracks.

A light came on. Sabry Bakr was standing beside her. Both were holding pistols trained on the Securitate officer.

"If he moves...shoot him," Sabry ordered. He went to the door leading to the tunnel. Glancing down, he could see the light coming toward the house through the tunnel.

"What have you been doing, Colonel?" Sabry asked. There was a meanness in his voice that Scornicesti had never heard before.

What followed during the next few moments was unclear to Scornicesti, except that he knew this was his only hope for survival.

The plate glass window shattered. Tiny shards of glass flew, striking Yasmin, who took the brunt of the hurricane-force wind that suddenly filled the room.

A thick cloud of hot, swirling dust enveloped them. Visibility was cut to zero.

There was only the sound of the wind blowing through the hole where the window once held out the night.

A wind that was drawing Scornicesti to its howl like light draws a moth. Only not to his death, he told himself.

With all his strength, Scornicesti forced his body through the obscuration toward the hole, breathing hot, bullet-like particles of sand.

The sound of a pistol shot was heard, though muffled. Distant.

He found the hole where the window had been. His hands gripped the frame. With all his strength he pulled against the howling tempest.

Glass cut at his hands. Another shot. He forgot the pain.

Scornicesti fell to the ground, stumbled forward, and righted himself. He knew the layout of the surrounding ground. Charging forward, he slammed against the gate. His fingers groped at the padlock.

Locked!

Without hesitation he jumped, gripped the upper rim of the gate and pulled himself over the top.

On the other side he began running; stumbling, falling, sometimes crawling, he didn't know where he was going. He only knew he couldn't go back.

Like a man lost in a dream, he was walking forward, his hands outstretched, as though feeling through the curtain of sand. His eyes burned from the agonizing dust and dirt; his nostrils were nearly filled as he forced himself forward.

The seconds passed into minutes and he felt the strength fading in his legs; his clothes were nearly stripped from his body. He looked like a long-forgotten scarecrow he had seen in a field near his boyhood farm in Romania.

Suddenly, he felt something. He was nearly knocked to the ground. His fingers felt the hardness of metal. Then clothing.

Squinting, he saw the outline of a man standing in front of him. Leaning closer, his eyes widened as the man appeared ghoulish, a terrifying apparition that looked like it came from hell.

The apparition had bulging metal eyes protruding from behind a cowl covering his head.

It has no eyes, he told himself.

He turned to run. He slammed into something else. Another ghoul. Again the metal, which he gripped, and recognized.

A rifle barrel.

Another appeared. Then another.

A hand reached out and grabbed Scornicesti. A ferocious hand that pulled with a strength the Romanian couldn't believe.

A strength greater than the sirocco. A strength he could only follow.

32

SACRETTE BENT FORWARD, PULLING ON THE LINE joining him to Farnsworth and Mostafavi. The compass was pressed under his nose, his only means of guidance.

That he suddenly crashed to the ground was no surprise. He had been stumbling and falling since leaving the mule.

What surprised him was that this time he didn't fall. He had been driven to the ground by a powerful force. One he didn't see. One that had risen suddenly from behind the pile of rocks near where he lay.

Breath nearly as hot as the sirocco burned in his ear.

"Captain Sacrette?"

Sacrette nodded to the strange-looking vision two inches from his face. A vision that looked like it came from another planet. Tubes were jutting from where eyeballs would be found on a human being. Had he not recognized the device he might have fought. But he knew that would be useless. The grip of his captor held him pinned firmly to the ground.

"Yes. I'm Sacrette. Who are you?"

"I've been instructed to bring you back to the carrier, sir," said the voice.

"Like hell," Sacrette replied.

Then he saw the black muzzle of a weapon perched on the end of his nose.

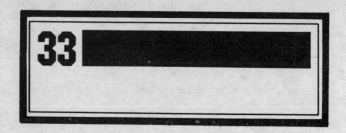

33

THE HOWLING WIND DIED WITH THE SUDDENNESS with which it had come. An eerie calm followed as the desert began settling to a restful state.

Marine Force Recon Lieutenant Clay Dunstan peeled off his NVG-2 night vision goggles. In the moonlight, Sacrette could see the camouflage around his eyes. Crusted sand coated his skin around where the goggles had covered his face.

Holding a USAS-12 automatic shotgun with a twenty-four-round drum, Sacrette could sense that the young officer was in no mood for bullshit.

"Those are my orders, Captain. Now move. We've got a helo inbound for an extract."

Before Sacrette could protest, he heard a voice with an unmistakable foreign accent.

Scornicesti pushed himself up to face the two officers. "We have to get out of here. They'll be looking for me."

After encountering Dunstan and his three Recon specialists, he gamely followed, knowing that with the Americans his chances were better than with the desert. Or the *Hafiza*. Besides, it was the Americans who could save him.

Especially now. His bargaining power had become enhanced by the knowledge he had. Knowledge they would want.

"Who the hell is he?" Sacrette was pointing at the Romanian.

Dunstan shrugged. "He claims he's a Romanian. Taken hostage by the terrorists who kidnapped Admiral Lord."

Sacrette got in front of the Romanian's face. "Have you seen an American admiral?"

Scornicesti snapped to attention and answered. "He was in the cell next to mine."

"Where is he being held?"

"In the dungeon. The dungeon of Kims. Beneath the monastery."

Suspicion filled Sacrette's face. "How did you escape?"

"The old man. The one they call Hakim. Hakim al-Sabbah Bakr. He had me brought from the dungeon for interrogation in the house. The storm damaged the house. I escaped."

Mohammad stepped forward. "Did you say 'al-Sabbah?'"

"Yes. He is the head of a group of fanatics. They are called..."

"The *Hafiza*," Sacrette finished the sentence.

Mohammad added what they already knew. "And the one called Hakim. He has added 'al-Sabbah' to his name. He is now the annointed 'Old Man of the Mountain.'"

"I don't care if he's the Ayatollah in drag," quipped Dunstan. "We're moving." He motioned one of his men to take the point.

"Wait a minute, Lieutenant. We can get Admiral Lord. This man knows where he's being held." Sacrette's hand was sliding to a pistol holstered on his hip.

Dunstan eyed the move. He stepped in close, then whispered. "I'm to either bring you back alive, or bury you here in the desert. It's your call."

Sacrette slowly lowered his hand. "You've got a lot of hard bark on your young ass, son."

"Yes, sir. I'm Force Recon. We come packaged that way!"

PART FOUR: ███████ NEAR STEEL BEACH

34

0800.

"I HOPE THERE'RE NO HARD FEELINGS, CAPTAIN. I WAS just following orders," said Lieutenant Dunstan. He was sitting near the opened door of the SH-60B Seahawk transporting the Americans, and one Romanian, to the aircraft carrier *Valiant*.

There was an uncomfortable pause, then Dunstan added, "For what it's worth, there's not a man on my team that wouldn't have backed you under any other circumstances. We know you would have done the same for us."

"No hard feelings, Lieutenant. You and your men did an excellent job."

Sitting beside him, Farnsworth was chewing on a Cuban cigar. "Goddamn the luck. We were that close." He held up his hand, touching the first digit on his index finger.

"Close only counts in horseshoes and hand grenades, Chief." Sacrette released a long sigh, then asked, "You got any plans for retirement?"

Farnsworth laughed. "Shit. I'm a chief petty officer in this man's navy. They ain't going to court-martial me. I know where there're too many dead bodies."

Sacrette didn't look so secure. He started to speak when he felt the helo begin to descend. That's when Dunstan pointed out of the opened door.

"Man. Look at this, Captain Sacrette. Everything but the kitchen sink and a brass band."

Sacrette knelt by the door. In the distance the aircraft carrier was in full view.

He felt a tug at his heart. Not from the airplanes parked in neat rows. Not the flag flying from above the island.

He saw them filling the flight deck.

Six thousand men of the USS *Valiant* had left their stations to greet the CAG.

Farnsworth sounded a little choked as he said, "I guess it's their way saying of 'you're not alone.'"

The helo was met by six burly Marines led by a young officer. Dressed in blues, the officer nodded at his men and a human envelope surrounded the two naval men.

Mostafavi was led to a waiting helicopter flown by the Royal police. He wasn't concerned for his freedom; he had not violated any law. Besides, two of the policemen in the helo were customers to whom he had sold weapons.

Scornicesti was taken by the officer to Captain Purcell.

Sacrette was led to his quarters. Farnsworth was taken to the CPO's bay. Both were followed by two Marines.

In his quarters, Sacrette turned on the shower to full Zone Five. He stepped into the steaming water gripping a bottle of Jack Daniels. After four big belts, he began to feel better, but only slightly. Fatigue. And failure was working on him. Not to mention half a fifth of whiskey.

Stepping from the shower, he found Domino sitting on his bunk. A tray of food was on the desk.

Sacrette's face instantly lit up when the smell struck his senses.

Handing the bottle out to Dom, Sacrette pulled back a white cloth covering a metal bowl filled with steaming shrimp.

"The spoons in the officer's mess wanted you to know they were thinking about you. They prepared the shrimp to your particular taste. Disgusting as it may be."

Sacrette clapped his hands loudly. "Boiled in orange juice. The juice gives the shrimp a flavor you can't believe. Try one, Dom."

Domino appeared ready to vomit. "No, thanks. I'll stick to boiling mine in water."

That's when Sacrette looked up and noticed something unusual about the exec's eyes. They were puffy; appearing strained. "What's wrong with your eyes? You look like a frog."

Domino automatically rubbed his eyelids, then shrugged. "Tired, you son of a bitch. I've been up all night. The whole carrier's been up. Waiting. Waiting to see if you were dead or alive. You and the admiral."

Sacrette stopped peeling the shell from a shrimp. He dropped the shrimp onto the tray. "Goddamn, Dom. We were so close. So damn close."

Domino nodded. "I know. But even if you had gotten into the monastery, you don't know where they're holding the admiral."

Sacrette stared hard at the exec. "There's someone who does know. And I intend to talk to him directly."

"The Romanian?"

Sacrette returned to the shrimp. "The Romanian. There's something about that character that's very un-kosher."

"I think you may be right. The skinny going around the boat is that he's asked for political asylum."

"Where are they keeping him?"

Domino laughed. "Sick bay. He complained about a bad back."

Sacrette frowned. "He belongs in the brig. Which is probably where I'll be after Purcell gets through with me."

Domino shook his head. "He wouldn't dare."

35

0900.

SACRETTE AND FARNSWORTH WERE FRESHLY SHOW-ered and shaved. Wearing dress whites, they stood at ramrod attention listening to the indictment they knew might be read when they had entered Iran.

"Insubordination. Absent without leave. Entering a foreign country hostile to the United States without authorization. Not to mention jeopardizing the political integrity of the United States." Purcell continued, reading the remainder of the charges.

"Gentlemen, you will stand a general court-martial. I promise you that. In the meantime, you will await transport to Fleet Headquarters under close arrest."

Purcell nodded to a Marine Corps security policeman standing near the door. "Put them in the brig!"

36

AN HOUR LATER, EVERYTHING THAT COULD POSSIBLY go wrong aboard the USS *Valiant* was going wrong.

Light bulbs were unscrewed in all the lighting fixtures.

Eight pounds of salt had been dumped into the food in the forward mess hall.

Dozens of aircraft were suddenly being reported as having parts missing.

Heavy machinery sat idle on the flight and hangar deck.

Vital personnel were nowhere to be found.

A mysterious radio no one could, or would locate, was blaring heavy metal music over the 1-MC carrier loudspeaker.

On the bridge, Captain Purcell heard the same nightmares from captains aboard other ships in the Battle Group. From the air wing exec, Commander Dominolli, he heard the word most dreaded by a ship's captain.

"Mutiny."

"Mutiny!" Purcell roared. He was walking in circles with his hands thrust deep in his pockets.

"That's the ticket, sir. The men are hotter than a whore's breath. If you don't do something soon, you're going to be in the deep *kim chi*. That's a fact, Captain. You can put me in the brig for being blunt, sir. I know you can. But there's something that has to be said. You're losing your ship because you're thinking with your ass."

"You're walking on very thin ice, Domino. Twenty years of friendship doesn't buy this sort of candor."

"It damn well better, Freeman." He pointed toward the flight deck. "That man is the CAG, for Chrissake. He's the commander of over thirty-five hundred men on this carrier. And hundreds more throughout the Battle Group. There's not a one of them that wouldn't jump through fire for Thunderbolt."

"I won't be intimidated by Captain Sacrette."

Domino shook his head. "Hell's bells, Freeman. He's not intimidating you. He's the last man who would condone this kind of action by these men. But they know if it had been their butts hanging in the fire, Sacrette would have been the first one off the flight deck. Like he was. Orders or no orders. And that includes your ass, as well."

Before he could respond, Purcell saw Lt. Commander Frederick Enoch enter, looking haggard. Enoch was the honcho of Damage Control.

"What's your problem?" Purcell snapped.

"Goddammit, sir. We've got a flood belowdecks. Every goddamned mother-loving toilet on the carrier has been stuffed with a goddamned towel and flushed. We've got enough goddamned water running in the passageways to float a goddamned battleship. You've got to do something, sir!"

Purcell turned to Domino.

Domino couldn't help but laugh. Purcell looked like a man with his dick caught in the shower door.

37

FARNSWORTH TURNED THE BOTTLE OF JACK DANIELS Old Number Seven to twelve o'clock high. He took a long pull, then handed the bourbon to Sacrette. The CAG took a long, slow swig, then rolled the bottled between his palms.

"Helluva way to end a career, Chief."

Farnsworth laughed. "Sit tight, Thunderman. The troops are on the move. I can feel it in these old bones." Farnsworth reached for the bottle.

A young Marine standing outside the cell stared angrily through the bars at the two sailors. "That's right, Thunderbolt. Captain Purcell is getting his comeuppance. And it ain't very pretty."

Sacrette rose and went to the bars. He looked suspiciously at the corporal. "What are you talking about?"

The corporal only grinned. He looked at Farnsworth. "Diamonds. What in hell is going on?"

Farnsworth held the bottle to the light. He eyed what Bourbon was left through the light fixture in the ceiling. A sly smile filled his face; it was as though he knew the light fixture was one of the few still operational aboard the carrier.

"The USS *Valiant* is now the USS *Clusterfuck*, Thunderman."

Seconds later, Captain Purcell entered the brig.

Farnsworth laughed when he saw what was in the exec's hand:

Purcell was carrying a flashlight.

38

ADMIRAL ELROD LORD BEGAN THE TEDIOUS TASK OF getting into the front seat of his F-4 Phantom. It was dark. He could see nothing. The crew was not there. There was silence.

He had done it hundreds of time. He always said he could get in the cockpit blindfolded.

Time to find out. He did it from memory.

Standing on the seat he completed the last detail before easing himself into the glove-tight Martin-Baker ejection seat: he zipped the right and left leg zippers of his speed jeans, eliminating the last bit of slack. The g-suit was tight. He slid his hand into the waist band to be certain. One snugly fit hand meant a good fit.

The first task upon easing into the seat was to connect leg restraints to his legs. One restraint over each knee; one above the top of each boot. During the ejection the trolley connected to the restraints would pull his legs back tight against the seat, preventing his legs from being sheared off at the knees should they strike the lip of the cockpit.

He connected the lap belt, then secured the survival seat to his torso harness.

Lugs on the parachute risers were next, also with a

quick connection to the torso harness.

Then he connected his oxygen/communication hose. Then the g-suit hose.

Mask onto his face. Check for breathing malfunction. Check for leaks along the nose area that might blow air into the eyes, which could quickly dry out the eyes during flight.

Connect commo line to mouthpiece.

Radio check.

Close canopy. Lock canopy. Shoulder harness lock lever forward to LOCK. Visor down over the eyes.

Prepare for catapult launch. Assume ejection position in the event of aircraft malfunction during take-off run.

Head back firm against headrest with chin elevated ten degrees. Shoulders and back firmly against seat back. Thighs pressed against side of seat. Heels flat on the deck with feet on rudder pedals.

Smart salute.

Launch!

Through the darkness of the dungeon cell he felt himself slam back into the seat under the force of twenty transverse g's.

He was free!

Flying high over the desert, Lord quickly rid his mind of the terror, of the impotence of capture.

He had launched six times since Hakim's visit. Each entry into the aircraft had been painstakingly thorough.

Each launch another escape from the dungeons of Kim.

"Mind over matter," he called to the darkness. "Mind over matter. I don't mind . . . you don't matter. You can't break me. I've been here before. I'll win.

Perhaps I'll die. But you won't break me."

As if to reassure the walls of his resolve, he said it again.

"I will win!"

He mentally gripped the stick, rolled left, standing hard on the left rudder. Outside the cockpit, he saw the wing roots light up with condensation as he bat-turned onto the target.

He was flying. Unafraid.

And then there was light. The door cracked slightly, then slowly creaked open. He didn't want to look, but he knew it was something he had to do.

There was no place to run. Nowhere to hide. He was alone.

Glancing to the door, he saw a tall figure dressed in a flowing robe step through the light bleeding from the hallway.

Again left rudder. He got the nose of the F-4 Phantom on the tall bedouin. He squeezed the trigger.

The bedouin dissolved.

In his mind.

"You have been summoned," said the voice. In his hand the tall sentinel held what looked like a long spear. Lord recognized the eleventh century halberd. The type carried by the Crusaders.

Slowly, he stood. He tightened his shoulders back, square and rigid.

Without a word, the Battle Group commander marched briskly through the door. His gray eyes were set straight ahead.

He had already determined he would die before showing fear.

He was the leader of fighting men and fighting ships.

He knew how to die.

39

"THE ROMANIAN IS NOWHERE TO BE FOUND. OUR MEN have searched the village. He is gone. Swallowed by the desert." Sabry Bakr explained to his father and the old men of the *Hafiza*.

A silence filled the prayer room. Silence and disappointment.

"Where will we get the weapons, Hakim? Without the Romanian we cannot help our brothers in Azerbaijan," said one of the mullahs.

Hakim waved his hand as though the question was not important. "Allah will show us the way. For now, we have other matters that require our attention."

One of the mullahs clapped his hands.

The door opened and the tall bedouin entered. He was carrying the halberd in one hand. In his other hand he held a rope.

A tug on the rope brought Admiral Elrod Lord stumbling into the room. His eyes were covered with a white blindfold. Blood stained the blindfold above his left ear.

"You have been summoned before the *Hafiza* to stand judgment," said Hakim. He nodded at the bedouin.

The blindfold was ripped from Lord's face. The

suddenness of sunlight caused Lord to squint but he quickly recovered and faced his accusers.

"On what charge?" demanded Lord.

"The death of Abdullaran Bakr. My son," Hakim replied in a firm voice.

Sabry Bakr was standing near the window. He glared evilly at Lord. Yasmin stood at his side. She wore a smug grin.

"I did not kill your son."

Hakim shrugged slightly. "Were you the commander of an American aircraft carrier in the Persian Gulf in June of 1985?" asked Hakim.

"You know I was."

"Did one of your men engage Captain Abdullaran Bakr in an aerial battle?"

"One of my men engaged an Iranian aircraft with hostile intentions. It was an act of self-defense."

"Was your country being attacked?"

"No. A helpless oil tanker was being attacked. We merely did what any civilized nation would do. We gave assistance. Your son initiated the attack."

"No!" Hakim shouted. "You interfered. You interfered with matters that did not concern you. That interference brought about the death of Captain Bakr."

Lord could see there was no logical way of reasoning with the man. "You have already made your decision. Why do you flatter yourself with this kangaroo trial? Go ahead and do whatever you have planned. I won't lend credence to this farce any longer. I've said what I said. It was war. But I will say this . . . your son was given every opportunity to withdraw. He chose to fight. He died like a man. You shame his memory with your cowardice."

Sabry lunged at the admiral. His fist crashed against Lord's cheek, driving him to the floor.

On his knees, Lord looked up at the younger Bakr. "I've had about enough from you, sonny boy."

He let it all hang out.

Lord's fist shot straight out, connecting in Sabry's groin. The movement was so quick, so unexpected, everyone in the room sat dumbfounded. Including the bedouin.

Sabry screamed. Clutching his testicles, he fell to his knees. Lord's index and middle fingers were curled into two, tight spikes. They drove for the soft tissue beside the larynx.

Sabry pitched back; Lord flew through the air, straddling his stunned assailant.

Within seconds the old men were on their feet. The bedouin charged forward.

The halberd swung in a high arc striking the admiral at the left temple.

Lord pitched onto his side. He lay unconscious.

His mouth was closed tight, but spread slightly. He appeared to be smiling.

40

SACRETTE WAS IN THE PRI-FLY TOWER TWO LEVELS above the Bridge at the aft portion of the island. The pri-fly tower is where the Air Boss conducts launch, recovery, fueling, and flight patterns of the carrier's aircraft.

Standing at the window, Commander Enoch Vestral, the air boss, had his hand over the catapult abort button. This was done on every launch. Should the air boss see something isn't kosher, something the launch crew may have missed, he can stop a launch even the catapult officer has given the launch signal.

While most of the personnel preferred watching launch and recovery from the 'buzzard's perch,' an observation deck on the top of the island, Sacrette preferred the pri-fly tower.

He didn't like to merely watch what was happening on the flight deck; he liked to hear what was happening. Most communication on the deck was by hand signal due to excess noise. In the pri-fly he could monitor voice communications between pilot and air boss.

The roar of an E2-Hawkeye shook the deck as the miniature AWAC thundered from the waist cat and lifted into the sky. The heavy discus-shaped rotodome mounted on top of the fuselage suggests the Hawkeye should develop too much parasitic drag to successfully get airborne from the carrier. That's not the case. The saucer shape of the rotodome effectively creates lift, neutralizing the drag.

Sacrette watched the strange looking craft rise slowly, gain airspeed, then depart the pattern.

There was a look of momentary satisfaction on Vestral's face as the Hawkeye began to fade northwest of the carrier. "She's en route to her station in Saudi Arabia, Thunderbolt. If the Iraqis *do* launch a missile, the Hawkeye will pick up the target first, then track the missile. We'll have height, range, and trajectory before they do."

Sacrette appeared pleased. Normally, aircraft are not launched from a carrier sitting in anchorage, nor from a carrier sitting in a foreign port. This case was an exception. One that required flexibility.

Much the way Purcell had become flexible by dropping the charges against Sacrette and Farnsworth.

Sacrette clapped Vestral on the shoulder. "Sorry to interrupt your shore leave, Enoch. Good job."

Vestral extended his hand. He was wearing a Cheshire grin. "Good to see you back in the saddle, Thunderbolt."

The CAG left the bridge and went to his office on the hangar deck. Paperwork was four inches deep on his desk. He began by checking with Maintenance Control for an update on his pilots' performance over the past week.

Pilot scoring ranged from "okay," a green pass, or damn near perfect, through "fair," "no grade," or a "cut" pass, which meant a landing so unsafe it could result in a crash.

All the ratings were mostly "okay," with one rated

"no grade." Nine times. That was the one that bothered him. Especially when he saw the name and reexamined the landings on the PLAT, the pilot landing aid television that films pilots' landings.

He watched the PLAT several times, then picked up the phone and called the ready room.

That's when he remembered something that had happened earlier while he was eating shrimp boiled in orange juice.

The pilot was summoned, and while he waited, Sacrette tried to think of what he was going to say.

When the knock came at the door he took a deep breath and called, "Enter."

The pilot stuck his head through the door. There was a big grin on his face. "How's the jailbird?"

Sacrette laughed, then motioned the pilot into his office. "Have a chair, Domino."

41

"EVERY CARRIER PILOT HAS A "TURN IN THE BARREL," Boulton. You know that. It's happened to you before. It happens to the best." The dark-eyed Italian from Brooklyn was referring to those occasions when a pilot couldn't get his aircraft onto the deck. Leaning back in his chair, he lit a cigarette, then set his Marlboros and Zippo lighter on the desk.

Sacrette nodded in agreement. He ran the PLAT again for Domino. The night Sacrette was aboard the *Kiev*, Domino had been on night patrol. Returning to the carrier, he made pass after aborted pass. Finally, on the tenth attempt he safely trapped on the flight deck.

Sacrette smiled sympathetically. He knew it was the truth. It had happened to him. Weather conditions on the surface could make a carrier landing nearly impossible. For Domino, that wasn't the case.

"I know, Dom. But dammit, man, the seas were calm. The wind was flat."

Domino shrugged. "It happens."

Sacrette reached across the desk and picked up the lighter. Miniaturized gold wings of the naval aviator were on the cover. Suddenly, without warning, he pitched the lighter to Domino.

The lighter bounced off the exec's chest, then fell to the floor. His hands never moved from his lap.

The metallic ring of the lighter hitting the deck summarized the CAG's argument. And his suspicion.

"What's wrong with your eyes, Dom?"

Domino leaned and picked up the lighter. "Not a goddamned thing."

Sacrette expected him to be defensive. All pilots were defensive when it came to criticism regarding their flying. Sacrette was the same way.

The CAG shook his head. "When was the last time the flight surgeon gave you an eye examination?"

Domino shrugged. "Six months ago."

Sacrette reached into his desk drawer. He removed the form all pilots despised. And feared. "I'm grounding you until you have a complete physical. Specifically— an eye examination." He began filling in the blanks.

Domino bolted to his feet. "That's a cheap shot, Captain."

Sacrette continued to write while he talked. "I can't take the chance, Domino. You're in command of a forty-million dollar aircraft and a naval flight officer. Not to mention landing aboard a billion-dollar aircraft carrier with a flight deck filled with men and equipment."

Sacrette pointed at the PLAT. "Six months ago you could have made that landing in a hurricane. Look at your approaches. You were coming in high on every pass. That suggests to me you weren't getting the ball focused until you were nearly over the deck."

Sacrette continued filling in the grounding form. Before he could say another word Domino turned and stormed out of the CAG's office.

Dropping his pen on his desk, Sacrette leaned back

in his chair. His eyes were vacant.

He ran the PLAT again.

The evidence was clear. He signed the grounding form.

And in doing so, knew he had lost a good friend.

42

1400.

WHEN THE CARRIER IS IN PORT, OR ON A STAND-DOWN at sea, the flight deck is turned into a massive sunning platform the sailors of the carrier call "Steel Beach."

Thousands of men lay stretched out beneath the sun on folding lounges and beach towels, soaking up the rays. Small children's swimming pools rested beneath the folded wings of A-7 Corsairs; volleyball nets were strung between parked aircraft. Music blared over the 5-MC flight deck loudspeaker from the carrier's radio station.

Shore leave had been cancelled by Captain Purcell should the mission against Iraq be given the green light.

That possibility was the only salvation that kept the men from complaining. The thought of going on the offensive was more entertaining than hitting the waterfront bistros and bars of Kuwait City.

The sky was clear of air traffic; all the aircraft were either parked on the flight deck or in the hangar deck.

With two exceptions. The E2 Hawkeye on patrol over the Saudi Arabian desert near the Iraq border, and the SH-60 Seahawk that was inbound from the airport with its special cargo.

The moment the helo appeared, the men paused from whatever they were doing, shaded their eyes against the bright sun, and watched while the helo landed.

When six men offloaded carrying their heavy rucksacks and weapons, thousands of pulses began to quicken on Steel Beach.

All eyes followed the men, who were led by a tall, rawboned Marine officer many recognized from previous missions.

Major Deke Slattery swaggered along the flight deck toward the island, carrying his heavy gear with the ease of a mother carrying her newborn child.

As the men disappeared through the hatchway of the island, Steel Beach began to buzz with speculation.

Speculation always ensued with the arrival of the SEALs.

Especially this team.

The elite of the elite.

Red Cell Six.

43

CPO DIAMONDS FARNSWORTH WAS SITTING ON HIS bunk in the CPOs' bay. Unlike the lesser-rated enlisted bays, which were one-hundred-bed sleeping areas labeled the "animal coop," CPO bays were more lavish.

More. But not by much. The CPO bays only housed forty chiefs.

Diamonds was sitting on the edge of his bunk, closing the lid on his "coffin locker," a foot locker for personal belongings.

"Diamonds. My main man. How they hanging?" A rough, husky voice called.

Farnsworth didn't have to look up. He would know the voice anywhere.

Marine Corps Gunnery Sergeant Franklin "Gunny" Holden was approaching wearing a huge grin. Dressed in camouflage fatigues, he carried an overburdened Alice pack stuffed with his gear in one hand. In the other he carried a 7.62 caliber SAW machinegun.

Walking behind him were four enlisted men. He recognized each of the men from Malta, and the year before when the SEALs were called in to assist in a Mediterranean terrorist situation.

Private Jesus "Tico" Madrid was a tough Chicano

kid from East Los Angeles. Around his neck was a wire saw that he could quickly turn into a deadly garrote. He was carrying his Alice pack and M-16. From his shoulder hung a heavy duffel bag, a bag Farnsworth knew was loaded with Madrid's "toys," deadly explosive devices that were brilliantly conceived.

Navy Corpsman Francis "Doc" Jerome, the team medic, carried a rifle gurney. Inside the gurney was a 7mm magnum high-powered rifle mounted with a STAR-LIGHT scope and long tubular silencer.

Besides his M-16, Lance Corporal Sam Phillips carried a smaller pouch. A pouch concealing a scope-mounted Barnett Commando crossbow. The 180-foot-pounds of killing machine could put a razor-tipped quarrel through a three-inch piece of wood. On his muscular forearm, resting in a black scabbard, was a Sykes-Fairburn fighting commando knife.

Finally, there was the most unique looking member of the group, although not at this moment, since his eyes were covered by specially treated sunglasses to block out both natural and artificial light. When the glasses were removed, Machinist Mate Conrad "Starlight" Gunnison's eyes were as white as snow. Including the pupils. He was one of the one-in-eighty-million born with the ability to see nearly perfectly in the dark. Gunnison was the point specialist. Especially during night ops.

"Loose and full of juice!" Farnsworth fired back. The two black men shook hands.

"You remember my children, don't you?" Gunny Holden jerked his thumb at the other enlisted men in Red Cell Six.

They all shook hands with Farnsworth then dropped their gear on the floor.

Farnsworth eyed the equipment. A sly grin stretched across his mouth. "You boys going to make some noise, Gunny?"

Holden shrugged.

"Like maybe go in and get the admiral?"

Holden shook his head. "Not the admiral, Diamonds. We're on alert status. We're just here in case we're needed."

Farnsworth had been told about the Iraqi missile complex by Sacrette. He wasn't able to hide the disappointment. "Damn. When I saw you I thought maybe..." His voice faded off.

Gunny slapped the chief on the shoulder. "He's a tough man, Diamonds. A tough sailor. He'll come through."

Diamonds released a long, slow sigh. He opened the coffin locker and took out a bottle of Scotch. "You fellows need to clear the rotor dust out of your pipes."

Each man took a long pull on the bottle. They looked tired. But ready to fight.

Before Diamonds stowed the Scotch, he raised the bottle to the elite commando special ops team.

"To the best of the best."

44

ADMIRAL LORD THOUGHT HE SAW A BEAUTIFUL YOUNG woman walking through the desert heat waves rising above the Iranian desert south of the mosque. She was tall. Slender. With long blond hair.

Then, as suddenly as she came, she disappeared. And he was alone.

His hands ached from the rope holding his wrists to two metal rings imbedded in the masonry between two of the five columns supporting the roof of the minaret. Below lay the courtyard surrounding the monastery of Kims.

From somewhere close he could hear the soft sound of prayer.

His feet were bare, as was his chest and the rest of his body, except his groin, which was covered by his boxer shorts.

He had been standing in the sun for several hours; how long he wasn't sure, but judging by the track of the sun he was unconscious long after the *Hafiza* suspended him from the place where they intended his life to end.

Slowly. By starvation. The sun would rise and set. He would know the torturing heat of day. The biting cold of desert night.

Water would be given. Just enough to keep him from dying of dehydration. That would be faster than what they planned for the man the *Hafiza* judged responsible for the death of Abdullaran Bakr.

He tried to keep his mind off dying by again mentally flying his Phantom. Over and over he flew. Each flight took him farther from the mosque.

Up. High into the clouds in a pure afterburner climb. Forgetting the parched agony in his throat. The cutting ropes.

Up. To the sky. Where something strange suddenly appeared through clouds at the edge of the atmosphere.

He saw a face. A gentle face. Long hair hung from his shoulders. There was a calm in the eyes of the gentle face. A calm that transmitted into the soul of Admiral Lord.

It was as though He understood.

As though He had been where Lord stood. Tortured above a cruel Arab desert.

And then Admiral Elrod Lord sagged beneath the ropes, as he had seen pictures of Him sagging from the ropes holding Him to the crucifix.

45

DOMINO LAY STARING AT THE BIRD CAGE HANGING from the ceiling of his personal quarters. Two brightly colored canaries sat on narrow perches on opposite sides of the cage.

Jester, the blue and black canary, was eyeing Flash, the green and red canary, with the same evil eye he had used on all his former roommates.

Jester was a gift from his youngest son. Domino kept the birds to remind him of family.

Ornery as hell, Jester had killed two previous roommates by pecking them to death. Against his better judgment, Domino kept giving the bird a new roommate, hoping each time that the new canary would survive.

After all, as he told Jester each time a new bird was slipped into the cage, no animal should be alone.

Not even a mean-assed bird.

Then he knew it was time to take care of more pressing matters. He rose and left his quarters, following the passageway through bulkhead after bulkhead until he reached a door he had avoided for months.

After forcing himself through the door of the sick bay, he glanced around, looking for Commander Lowell Holwegner, the flight surgeon.

Instead, he saw Captain Boulton Sacrette and a Marine Corps major he instantly recognized.

Domino ignored Sacrette. To Slattery, he extended his hand and greeted the SEAL.

"What are you doing here, Deke?" Domino asked.

Slattery nodded at a closed door. "I want to talk to your guest."

Without further word, Slattery pushed the door open and entered the room. Sacrette followed.

Through the door, Domino saw two large Marines standing by a single bed. Sitting on the edge of the bed in a hospital gown was a man he recognized.

Colonel Gheorge Scornicesti.

46

"YOU'RE NOT SITTING IN THE CATBIRD SEAT LIKE YOU think, Colonel." Sacrette warned the Romanian. He held up a sheet of computer printout paper.

"What is that?" Scornicesti asked. He was lighting a cigarette while looking over the flame at the page.

"Your story sounded a little too shaky. So we've done some checking. Your country is in a shambles, but our embassy was able to get a line in the water to one of your people in the new government." He tapped the page menacingly against the flat of his hand.

"You're quite well known, Colonel," said Slattery. There was a hard edge to his voice.

Scornicesti adjusted the gown and took a long pull from the cigarette. "I am a political refugee. I am seeking asylum from your government. What else is there to know?"

"Not so fast. You're a refugee. That's for certain. One that has a lot of blood on his hands." Sacrette read from the communique. "Colonel Gheorge Scornicesti. Colonel in the now-defunct Romanian secret police, known as the Securitate. Personal aide to Iulian Vlad, former chief of the Securitate. It says you were his head of "special projects" for Middle East affairs. Specifically, arranging for the sale of Romanian Jews to the state of Israel. And, the conduit between the government of Romania and the Islamic Republic of Iran. Iran. Where we found your ass wandering through the desert."

Sacrette crushed the communique in his fist. "Now, Colonel Scornicesti, I suggest you start talking if you don't want me to put your ass in a helo and fly you back to that fucking monastery and drop your ass out from twenty thousand feet. Or, if you prefer, I'll take you to the Romanian embassy in Kuwait City. I'd bet a month's pay they'd love to get their hands on the likes of you. And you know what that means."

Slattery interrupted nonchalantly, but matter-of-factly. "The people your Securitate brutalized for decades have developed a sudden attractiveness for execution. If you get my drift."

Scornicesti said nothing for a long moment. Finally, he shrugged and appeared defeated. "What do you want?"

"The truth. Chapter and verse. Starting with what you were doing at that monastery, up to—and including—what you know about Admiral Lord. Especially Admiral Lord."

For the next thirty minutes Colonel Gheorge Scornicesti spilled his guts to the two Americans.

After hearing about the Azerbaijan plot, and getting the layout of the house and monastery, including information concerning the tunnel leading from the house to the dungeon, Slattery was confused about one point.

"If you knew the guns were in Romania, and you couldn't deliver the weapons, why did you go to the monastery? What was in it for you? Except the chance that you might have a pole shoved up your ass and be planted in the desert?"

A devious look filled Scornicesti's face. "Your admiral is not the only person the *Hafiza* are holding in the dungeon of Kims. There are four others. I intended to help them escape, then use them as a means to bargain my own political freedom."

Sacrette's face tightened into a hard mask. "When Admiral Lord arrived you switched gears, figuring it was easier to get one man out as compared to four. An American admiral would buy one hellava lot of political bargaining."

Scornicesti waved his hand casually. "They had been there for months. They were in poor health. Your admiral was stronger, and like you say, moving one man is easier than four."

"Where were you going to take him?"

"To Iraq. The border is not far away. When I went to get the admiral, that black-assed madman, Hakim al-Sabbah Bakr, was in the admiral's cell. I was discovered when I returned to the house. His son, and the woman called Yasmin, had become suspicious. Two crazy fanatics if two ever existed. They were going to kill me. I ran when the storm blew the front window apart."

Sacrette leaned into the face of the former Securitate agent. "Why were the four hostages in the cell important? Who were they?"

"Four military officers."

"What country?" snapped Slattery.

"The Soviet Union. They were flying in Azerbaijan, near the Iranian border when their plane was forced down. They were captured by members of the *Hafiza* and taken to the monastery for safekeeping. Until the revolution began in Azerbaijan."

"At which time they could be used as political pawns," said Slattery.

Sacrette didn't look convinced. "The Russians wouldn't exchange prisoners with the Azerbaijanis. Not for money. Or anything else."

Scornicesti laughed. "They would for one of the prisoners. He's a very important man."

"What's his name?" Sacrette demanded.

There was a pause, then Scornicesti said the name of a man Sacrette knew the Russians would pay to have released.

A name that would buy a great deal of political freedom.

"Air Marshal of the southern air defence—*Voyska Protivovozdushnoy Oborony*. Lieutenant General Pietor Andreyevich Zuberov."

Zuberov!

The father of Major Sergei Zuberov.

PART FIVE: OPERATION WAR CHARIOTS

47

1600.

FLYING AT ANGELS TWENTY-FOUR, THE CREW OF THE
E2C-Hawkeye had settled into their specific tasks. The
two-man flight crew flew the "Hummer," as it's called,
while the three systems specialists in the back operated
the instrumentation.

The most important of all the equipment was the
rotodome, the discus-shaped sensor housing the APA-
171 antennae mounted on top of the fuselage.

Turning one complete revolution every ten seconds
the scanner worked in conjunction with the APS-125
ARPS advanced radar processing system and ALR-59
passive system, enabling the Hawkeye to locate aircraft
at a distance of three hundred miles.

If the Hummer were flying over New York, the equipment could track and process radar information over an
area that would extend from Boston to Washington D.C.

With a capability to track more than 250 airborne
targets while simultaneously controlling the activity of
30 surface ships, the Hummer was truly the Battle
Group's "eyes in the sky."

Sitting in the left seat of the cockpit, Hummer pilot
Lt. Commander Darrel Jessup was flying a consistent pat-

tern west of the Saudi-Iraqi border. In the back, the systems operators were monitoring their screens while munching sandwiches from a "puke sack," a mess hall brown-bag lunch consisting of sandwiches, a fruit cup, and juice.

Air activity was slim to none when the screen lit up with four blips over what they knew was the missile complex at Al-Nasra.

"Something's coming off the ground, sir," called Lt. j.g. Eric Warner from his operator's chair.

The four blips identified were in two pairs, each in formation.

"Could be observation aircraft," said Warner, who pressed several digital buttons, relaying the real-time transmission to the CIC aboard the *Valiant*.

"Now," he whispered to himself. "Let's see if the fat lady sings."

Minutes later, another blip appeared. A single blip rising slow, as determined by the SLAR side looking radar.

The speed increased; the trajectory was constant.

"She's not an airplane, Commander Jessup. We've got a straight up target. A missile."

The missile increased in speed, rising through fifty thousand feet. Seventy-five thousand feet. One hundred thousand feet, where the trajectory changed, bringing the missile onto a southerly heading.

"That's the ticket. A hot rocket. An ICBM," said Warner. "Look at that mother go!"

The blip turned south, guided by ground control at the Al-Nasra missile complex.

Seconds later the missile disappeared downrange, out of the Hummer's tracking envelope.

Jessup was on the horn to the CIC. "Did you get that transmission, Home Plate?"

"Roger. Return to bird farm," the voice replied.

Jessup banked the Hawkeye to the southeast while telling his crew, "Catch some sack time on the way back to the barn. I have a feeling it's going to be a long night . . . and a long tomorrow."

48

OPERATION WAR CHARIOT JUMPED OFF WITH A CALL to the chairman of the Joint Chiefs. That was followed by a call to general quarters. At Captain Purcell's orders, the *Valiant* steamed out of Kuwait Bay. Personnel hurried to their duty stations and began preparing for the strike.

In the magazine, ordnance was broken out of storage lockers by ordnance personnel. Bombs were assembled and transported topside to the starboard side "bomb farm" aboard special bomb elevators.

Throughout the carrier the excitement built to near frenzy levels, then settled to professional calm as the minutes ticked away.

In the VFA 101 ready room, Captain Sacrette briefed the squadron commanders of the air wing.

Beaming from an overhead projector was the complex at Al-Nasra. Sacrette pointed at the airfield.

"Our mission is two-fold: neutralize the airfield and fly TAC CAP. This includes securing the highway to prevent the Iraqis from bringing in reinforcements. VFA 101 will conduct the mission in two modes: strike and fighter. I'll fly in the dual Strike/Fighter mode."

Sacrette looked at Lieutenant Ryan Michaels.

"Rhino. You'll lead the fighters in the TAC CAP. I'll lead the mud movers on the strike mission. If you need help I'll assist."

Rhino shifted uncomfortably in his chair. The word was out that Domino had been grounded. "What about refueling?"

"We'll tank with A-6's before reaching the coast. The A-6's will remain airborne to provide refueling during the operation. Refueling will be conducted in pairs. One taking the drink, the other providing stand-off cover."

When the briefing ended the pilots swaggered out of the ready room. Confidence was high. Sacrette noted there was some nervousness. That was expected. A nervousness that was somewhat shrouded by the traditional arrogance of the fighter pilot and RIO.

In the passageway, Sacrette saw Doc Holwegner approaching. He was carrying a medical chart.

"Doc. What's the skinny on Domino?"

Holwegner looked disappointed as he answered. "Cataracts."

Honest disappointment registered on the CAG's face. It was the kiss of death for a pilot. "Damn. What about surgery?"

"That's the next step. If that doesn't solve the problem, he'll be retired stateside. I'm shipping him to Bethesda after the mission. Along with any other injured personnel we may have."

Sacrette wanted to see his old friend, but he knew that would only cause Domino greater pain. A grounded pilot, especially the exec of a squadron preparing for a fight, doesn't want to be reminded he won't be in the fight.

Domino wouldn't want to see anyone. He shook hands with the flight surgeon and went to the flight deck.

An H-53 Sea Stallion was winding up its engines.

Major Deke Slattery was standing near the lowered rear ramp when Sacrette approached. He was wearing a parachute harness. His face was painted in desert camouflage, matching his fatigues, fatigues Sacrette knew were identical to those worn by the Iraqi army. He was talking to another Marine Corps officer Sacrette recognized from a previous encounter. The young officer was also dressed in desert camouflage and wore a parachute harness.

"Semper fi, Thunderbolt." His muzzle-flash smile was quick, to the point.

Sacrette nodded to Slattery.

"Captain," Lieutenant Clay Dunstan extended his powerful hand.

Sacrette grinned as he shook hands with the leader of the Force Recon team that would assist in the operation. "You're somewhat out of your element tonight, Lieutenant."

Dunstan's face set hard as concrete. "I don't understand what you mean, sir." He said 'sir' with a distinctive hard edge.

"It's my understanding that Force Recon is successful when it's never seen. Never heard. You boys are definitely gonna be seen . . . and heard tonight."

"That's our mission, Captain. Recon is quiet duty. We'll lay in the dark while the enemy shits on our sleeve. We won't say a word. Nor take a breath. But once in a while, we do get to make some noise." The hard features softened. "Tonight is one of those nights."

Sacrette winked at Slattery. The SEAL was beaming. He was a man who loved cockiness that could be backed up.

Sacrette said to Dunstan, "Good luck, Lieutenant."

To Slattery: "I understand you're taking along an extra man."

Slattery nodded mysteriously. "Yes, sir. A specialist. We had a helluva time finding one who fit the qualifications."

Sacrette didn't understand. "What qualifications?"

"We're working with the Russkies, so we'll need someone to interpret. Someone who speaks Russian. We'll be directing the air strike from the ground, which means they need forward observer training. Someone who can tell you guys the best ordnance to deposit into those damn SAM bunkers. Finally, someone with SEAL training. Parachute training."

Sacrette began to look uncomfortable. "That's a tall order. Did you find your man?"

Slattery jerked his thumb toward the interior of the Sea Stallion. "I found just the right man. And he has combat experience."

Sacrette stepped onto the ramp of the Sea Stallion. Five SEALs were crunched together with five Force Recon Marines. In the middle sat a man grinning through a fresh application of face camouflage.

"*Do'bree ve'cher*, Thunderbolt," CPO Diamonds Farnsworth greeted the CAG in flawless Russian.

49

1945.
Al-Nasra, Iraq.

THE MAIN GATE AT THE AL-NASRA MISSILE COMPLEX
was guarded by two Iraqi soldiers, men Amin Rushda
knew as well as his fat, ugly wife. Passing through the
gate he flashed his buff-colored badge, said hello, then
hurried along the narrow road leading to the main entrance of the complex.

Before him, looming tall from the desert floor stood
the mountain, a natural protective barrier.

Rushda moved hurriedly, much faster than usual.
His long, slender, brown fingers gripped an unexpected
treasure he had found that afternoon in his postal box.

Stopping, he again opened the manila envelope. He
glanced inside. The cover of a magazine gleamed, col-
orful and glossy, beneath the brilliant lights shining off
the SAM bunkers protecting the missile complex.

His breathing quickened. A beautiful face was all
he could see on the cover. The note inside telling him,
"For your reading pleasure."

It was signed by a name he didn't recognize. Perhaps
the postal delivery man made a mistake. He shrugged.
Someone else's loss was his good fortune.

He walked on, thinking about the joy he would

experience during tonight's shift. Dull. Boring. His work never changed.

He would sit there all night staring at the television screens displaying the front entrance that led into the underground missile complex.

Tonight would be different. Tonight there would be beautiful pictures to observe.

Truly, he thought, as he entered the opened door of the missile complex, *"There is a God in Heaven."*

Then the door closed, sealing the control operator in the tiny room where he operated the opening and closing of the entrance leading to the largest underground missile complex outside of the United States and the USSR.

50

THIRTY MINUTES AFTER DEPARTING THE USS *VALiant*, the H-53 was cutting through the clear night, skimming twenty feet above the Iraqi desert to avoid radar detection. The pilot wore night vision goggles; through the goggles the land appeared green.

Checking his digital map display on the instrument panel, the pilot changed course several times, following the crackback terrain changes. The flat terrain became hilly, then mountainous. Through the goggles he could see the land was barren except for a sprinkling of small shrubs jutting from between rocks.

"God. What an ugly fucking country," said Gunny Holden. He was wearing NVG's, as were all the commandos in the Sea Stallion. Watching the ground rush past, Gunny turned and nudged Farnsworth. "Are you going to be up to this, Diamonds? We've got a four-mile hump from the DZ to the missile complex."

Diamonds shoved a Cuban cigar into his mouth. "I can still outwalk your ass, son. You seem to have forgotten, I'm the one who taught you all you know about being a SEAL."

Gunny laughed. Turning to Starlight, he giggled as the man's white eyes appeared green through the night vision goggles. "Starlight, you look like a hoot owl."

Starlight's teeth gleamed behind a broad grin. "At least I don't have to wear one of those Star Wars contraptions." He glanced out the window. "Matter of fact . . . the moon is a little bright tonight." He slipped on his sunglasses, and to prove his value in the dark, took a Clive Cussler novel from his rucksack and began reading.

Ten minutes later the SEALs heard the engine noise fade as the pilot shifted to whisper mode.

Slattery was sitting near the ramp. Across from him was Lieutenant Dunstan. Both commandos were wearing internal commo headsets.

"Approaching the drop zone, Major Slattery," the pilot's voice crackled in Slattery's ear.

Slattery stood up and connected his static line to an anchorline cable running the length of the fuselage. Slattery's hook-up signaled the other SEALs and Farnsworth to their feet.

Rising, Dunstan hooked up his static line. His five Recon specialists pulled themselves to their feet and hooked up to the anchorline cable.

The electrical whir of the rear-ramp opening filled the fuselage; hot, dusty desert air swirled through the ramp way.

"Get them ready, Major," the pilot said.

The helo was five miles south of the missile complex. Flying through a valley carved through thousand-foot mountains, the pilot was preparing for the manuever that would give the SEALs and Force Recon team enough altitude for canopy deployment while maintaining radar avoidance.

"Here we go, brother," Gunny put out his hand.

Diamonds slapped a high-five, then flashed a thumbs up. "See you on the ground, Gunny."

Before Gunny could respond the men felt the increase in g-forces as the helo went into an abrupt steep climb.

Executing the "pop up," the pilot pressed a button at five hundred feet above the ground.

The interior of the Sea Stallion turned red but the commandos were already exiting the climbing helo.

One by one they stepped into the emptiness beyond the ramp. The ground below was a green haze through their NVG's as they felt the rotor wash push them toward the earth.

Unlike an airborne jump from a troop transport, in which the prop wash would thrust the jumper back and assist in the deployment of the canopy, a helo blast was significantly different.

The sensation of falling was only slight; canopy deployment was slower since the downward thrust of the rotor wash retarded, rather than assisted, in canopy deployment.

Falling in a tight paratrooper tuck, Farnsworth was counting. When he reached four, he felt the suspension lines begin to stretch. Canopy shock followed as the parachute opened.

Diamonds checked canopy, then released his PAE parachute assault equipment bag connected to his harness. The bag dropped and hung below his feet on a twenty-five foot static line.

As they neared the ground, the terrain appeared rocky. Diamonds put his feet together, bent his knees slightly, then waited for impact.

He hit the ground hard, but avoided injury with a

perfect PLF parachute landing fall.

Glancing around, he could see the other commandos were wrapping up their canopies and hiding them in the rocks.

Slattery found a clearing and hand-signaled the others to his position.

Kneeling on the hard, sun-baked sand, the SEAL leader was looking at a map. Dunstan came to his side. They spoke in whispers.

"We'll split up here. Our objective is the missile complex. From here we go north, straight over the mountain," Slattery's finger touched a valley on the south side of a small mountain range. "Here's our location." His finger crawled over the map to a point circled in red four miles north of the valley. "That's the missile complex."

Dunstan tapped a blue circle three miles west of the missile complex. "That's the airfield. Our target."

Slattery pushed the NVG's off his face. He looked around, but saw nothing. "Where in the hell are those bastards?"

Suddenly, the commandos stiffened at the sound of boot leather scruffing against rock.

Fingers coiled around triggers. All eyes turned to the side of the mountain. Through their goggles, the Americans saw twelve figures moving down the rocky slope.

Bent low, using the rocky formations for cover, the men traversed the slopes with the agility of mountain goats.

One by one they emerged from the rocks.

Slattery relaxed his finger around the trigger of his M-16.

The twelve men were dressed in desert camouflage

and carried heavy backpacks. Some carried RPG-7's; all carried AK-47 assault rifles. They, too, wore night vision goggles.

Spetsnaz. Russian commandos.

Most *spetsnaz* units were army, assigned to the GRU, Soviet military intelligence. Slattery had been briefed this *spetsnaz* unit was from the Soviet Naval Infantry, the elite of the Soviet navy as the SEALs were the elite of the American navy.

The two units were trained similarly, with very similar missions.

Spetsnaz had five primary missions: assassinating political enemies; attacking enemy nuclear installations; attacking command or communication centers; attacking key defense installations; and, attacking enemy power supplies.

Unlike Soviet and American airborne troops, *spetsnaz*, and their SEALs counterparts didn't wear distinctive berets.

Like the SEALs, *spetsnaz* preferred to keep their military identity from the enemy until it was too late.

Slattery watched the Russians with a certain uneasiness. Joint operation or no joint operation, he had tangled with Soviet *spetsnaz* in the past, in Grenada, during *Operation Urgent Fury*.

They were tough. Professional. Killers.

Like the SEALs.

But they were still Russians!

"Major Slattery?" A short, stocky officer was approaching, whispering Deke's name.

Slattery stepped forward. "Commander Harschenko?"

The two men eyed each other for a moment. Finally,

at the same moment, their hands extended.

The SEALs and Force Recon men greeted the *spetsnaz* with silent handshakes.

"You might say this is a historical moment, Major," Commander Harschenko commented. "For the first time since the Great War our two nations are joined together in a common military objective."

Slattery replied, "I hadn't thought about that, Commander. But I like the idea. We've been kicking the hell out of each other long enough." From his pocket he removed a can of Skoal. He dipped, put a pinch between his cheek and gum, then offered the tobacco to the Russian.

The Russian placed a pinch in his mouth, then removed a metallic flask from inside his camouflage battle jacket.

Slattery's face tightened at the sight of the flask.

Harschenko raised the flask in a toast to Slattery, then took a swig. *"Na zdorovie."*

Only after drinking first did he offer the flask to Slattery.

Slattery wasn't offended that the Russian drank first. All the men understood Slattery's suspicion. It was the Russian's way of telling Slattery the liquor was not poisoned, a favorite trick of *spetsnaz*.

Slattery smelled the flask. The smell was lemony. He recalled the name of the special vodka mixture. "I haven't tasted *pertsovka* in several years."

What he didn't say was that he first drank the liquor from a similar flask. One he removed from a dead *spetsnaz* in Grenada.

With the amenities dispensed with, the two military units discussed their plan.

"Commander Harschenko and five of his men will accompany the Recon team to the airfield." He looked at a young Soviet naval officer introduced as Lieutenant Arkady Belenkov. "Lieutenant Belenkov and five of his men will accompany me and my team to the missile complex."

Lieutenant Belenkov was tall; the way he easily handled his heavy backpack made him appear powerful. Slattery suspected the backpack was packed with explosives.

Without another word, the two commanding officers nodded sharply at their junior officers. Dunstan and his Force Recon team left with Harschenko and his men.

Belenkov and his *spetsnaz* left with Slattery and his SEALs.

At the base of the mountain the SEALs and Russians would climb, Farnsworth scanned upward toward the crest.

The climb looked backbreaking.

Harness straps were cutting into Farnsworth's shoulders. Sweat from the heat was pouring down his face.

And for the first time since climbing into the helo aboard the carrier, the CPO knew he was about to get his ass kicked for breaking the first rule of the military:

Never volunteer!

51

2300.

THE FLIGHT DECK OF AN ATTACK AIRCRAFT CARRIER during cyclic ops of a mission was a study in knowledge of an individual's particular duty and skills, the ability to operate under extreme pressure and, most importantly, chaos management.

With an aircraft launching every forty-five seconds, it took only one foul-up to turn the deck of a nuclear fighting complex into a three-ring circus.

Approximately forty aircraft were on deck at the same time; launches were conducted in pairs from the two catapults. One set was no sooner launched and clear than another set was launched; the empty cats were then readied for the next launch. Aircraft were rolled in front of the JBD jet blast deflector. The catapult officer checked the flaps to be certain they were properly set; launch bars were connected into the shuttlecock. The pilot was signaled to begin his engine run-up. At night, lights would go on.

The "button man," the catapult operator responsible for firing the cat, was setting the steam-driven catapult to the particular weight of a particular aircraft. The weight was chalked onto the fuselage. Weight was crucial; more important to a catapult officer and pilot than to Dolly Parton.

To use the same launch drive on the cats for each aircraft would have been catastrophic.

The power needed to throw a fully loaded F/A-18 Hornet in the strike mode at slightly over fifty thousand pounds could not be used on the same aircraft in the fighter mode at slightly over thirty thousands pounds.

To do so would have literally ripped the guts out of the Hornet with too much drive.

Conversely, to launch a striker with fighter drive would not throw the striker with enough power to become airborne.

The striker would simply wind up pitching over the end of the bow into the deep blue sea.

When all systems were go, the cat officer would check to be sure the pilot and RIO were sitting with their heads against the headrest to prevent whiplash. He would return the pilot's salute, then kneel, facing down the runway.

When all was ready, he'd point two fingers down the runway, the signal for the cat to be fired.

He would then lean forward, his head bent, shoulders hunkered down, as the aircraft vaulted forward, spewing a fire-hot breath of exhaust and backblast.

All other catapult personnel would remain behind the JBD. Protected by the steel barn-door size deflector.

It was a nervous business being a cat officer.

Oddly enough, most didn't drink heavily during off-duty hours. Some said they actually loved their jobs, kneeling there in that ferocious afterburner roar while the leading edge of an airplane's wing knifed past, only inches above their heads. They could see the safety wires in the bomb fuses; read the lettering on the missiles hanging from wing and fuselage hardpoints.

Taste the JP-4 jet fuel.

A taste that stayed with them until death at old age. Or on the flight deck.

Captain Boulton Sacrette loved the cat officers. On several occasions they were the difference between his living and dying. Bombs spotted hanging improperly; a tire too worn to survive cat shot and trap arrest.

Which was why Sacrette, an impatient man by nature, was sitting patiently in the cockpit of his F/A-18C night-configured Hornet locked in the tension of Cat One, where they were launching the heavier strikers.

He knew when the fingers pointed out the button would come down and he would have a better chance of surviving.

Lt. Rhino Michaels hadn't yet learned to appreciate patience of this caliber. He was a young fighter pilot. Young fighter pilots were not patient men, except when flying. He wasn't flying. He was sitting in Cat Two, where they were launching the fighters, waiting for the same two fingers. For the same button to be pressed.

He was waiting for something else, as well: his first time to go into real combat! Not the "Topgun" stuff, from where he graduated with honors. But the real thing.

Where second-place finishes are no finishes at all.

Then he saw the two fingers point down the cat.

The Hornet stormed down the catapult, then went over the edge.

There was the momentary weightlessness, the slight sinking sensation, then the power surge forward as the two engines began cooking through the sky.

Ten minutes later, high above the carrier, Rhino

spoke into his mouthpiece. "Blue Wolf one, to Red Wolf one." Rhino had been designated commander of the CAP TAC fighters, the Blue Wolf call sign.

Sacrette had Red Wolf, the strikers.

"Red Wolf one. Go."

"Red Wolf and four wolf cubs at Angels eighteen. Will tank when all fifteen cubs are in formation. Request you send the A-6's."

"Roger. A-6's en route. Red Wolf pack in formation. Will proceed to point Charlie and await your arrival."

Flying at Angels twenty, Sacrette banked left. Fourteen strikers followed his engine fire trails through the blackness above the Gulf.

Switching to another crypto frequency, Sacrette spoke to the USS *Minot*, referring to them by their callsign. "Golf Course . . . this is Wolf one. We are tripping the lights fantastic!"

Before the *Minot* communications officer could respond, Sacrette and his strikers had penetrated Iraqi airspace.

52

THE USS *MINOT* WAS CALLED "GOLF COURSE" DUE to the many helipads on the ship. Home of a Marine medium helicopter squadron, and six hundred cooped-up fighting jarheads, the *Minot* was buzzing with activity.

H-53 Sea Stallions, each carrying twenty-five battle-dressed Marines, waited for the order.

When Lieutenant Colonel Henderson, whose call sign was "Bayonet," gave the word, the sky above the *Minot* shook as wave after wave of giant Sea Stallions lifted off the decks.

Approaching the Iraqi border, the twenty-five helos were not alone.

"Bayonet... Blue Wolf one. Will provide TAC CAP to the LZ."

"Roger... Blue Wolf one. Proceeding to lima zulu. Appreciate your company."

The helicopter assault squadron penetrated Iraqi air space, nearly touching the desert. Wave after wave pushed through the darkness, guided by pilots wearing night vision goggles. Henderson kept his off. He preferred not to see the ground. He knew it was only a few feet below the deck of his helo.

He checked his watch.

2330.

Activity was popping all around the Iraqi border. Airborne troops were en route from their refueling stopover at Incirlik, Turkey, where the U.S. Air Force base was accommodating the Soviet paratroopers during the operation.

Carrier-based fighters and bombers were launching, moving into position to begin the footrace to Al-Nasra.

He wondered about Dunstan. The Recon officer was one of the best he had seen. It was his first action. He said a silent prayer.

Not for himself; he was a combat veteran. He knew his chances were good.

It was for his young marines. They would know their first taste of battle, and in doing so, would never be the same.

Life after combat was never the same.

Until the next fight.

53

2400.
Dayr Az Zawr Air Base, Syria.

MAJOR SERGEI ZUBEROV WALKED BRISKLY FROM THE exclusive Soviet ready room at Dayr Az Zawr air base to his waiting MiG-31 "Foxhound." The base, a training center for Syrian pilots, would be used by the Soviets during the operation. The Damascus government had objected at first. Those objections had ended when they learned that the Iraqis had ICBM capability. A capability that could bring Syria under the dominion of the Iraqis.

Climbing to the cockpit, Zuberov slipped on his helmet and buckled himself into the front seat. From the backseat, Captain Gennady Darkunin, the radar and electronics warfare systems officer, spoke clearly. "All systems ready. Ejection seat armed. Prepared for take-off."

Zuberov eased forward on the throttles of the Foxhound's twin Tumansky R-31F afterburning engines. Two red tongues burned from the exhaust nozzles as the newest plane in the Soviet Union's front line of defense rumbled along the yellow taxi-line leading to the runway.

Minutes later, the flight line at the air base shook as the Soviet tactical intercept squadron rolled onto the active runway in thundering pairs.

In less than six minutes, twenty-four of the supersonic stand-off interceptors were airborne.

In his cockpit, Zuberov switched to the special frequency selected for the mission.

"Red Wolf one . . . this is Red Star leader."

There was a pause, then Zuberov heard the voice of a man he expected to ultimately face in aerial combat, but never fight with in a common cause.

"Red Star leader . . . have you on radar." In his cockpit, Sacrette's radar showed twelve blips. The Sovs were flying in typical Soviet formation. They were flying tandem, one on top of the other. This tactic effectively made the force appear half its deadly size.

As his finger began to switch to the tactical frequency used by his squadron, Sacrette's voice called back again, this time with information the Soviet pilot knew was not part of the operation.

"Major Zuberov, I have information regarding four packages the Soviet Union recently lost in southern Azerbaijan."

Zuberov's heart nearly stopped. He understood, though Sacrette was talking cryptically. "Please explain, Captain."

Sacrette continued. "Be advised . . . four Soviet—and one American—packages are currently being stored in area south of 'dance floor' in neighboring country. In the basement. Will provide additional information at conclusion of 'dancecard.' "

Dancecard was the code name given the joint operation. Dance floor was the designation given the missile complex at Al-Nasra.

Monitoring the transmission from the backseat, Captain Darkunin understood as well. When the American and Soviet flight leaders broke off communication, Darkunin piped in, "Your father is alive, Sergei."

Behind the oxygen mask hooked to his helmet, a grin spread across Zuberov's face.

54

0010.

CODE NAMED "BALL ROOM," THE AIRFIELD AT AL-Nasra lay silent except for the occasional jeep moving along the flight line. Scanning the base through high-powered night vision binoculars, Lieutenant Clay Dunstan lay concealed in the desert sand near the base. An electrical fence was to the front; beyond the fence lay the flight line. Beside Dunstan lay Commander Harschenko.

Harschenko scanned the field through his glasses. He was carefully observing the primary target, a radar installation located beside the ops building on the flight line.

Dunstan was focusing on their secondary targets, which the Recon team was assigned to destroy.

"There are three barracks. Each barracks houses approximately one hundred men. Two of the barracks house troops from an infantry company responsible for security on the air base, and the missile complex. The third barracks houses the troops assigned to the SAM missile squadron at the missile complex. When the balloon goes up, we'll knock out the barracks. You have to give us time to set up."

Harschenko nodded. "Do you have your headsets?"

Dunstan took a small radio communicator from his rucksack. Each man in the force had an identical unit. Slipping the headset onto his close-cropped head, he adjusted the boom mike. The marines and *spetsnaz* lying nearby did the same.

After a quick radio check, the first step of the penetration began.

A *spetsnaz* trooper ran in a low crouch to the electrical fence. After neutralizing the electricity with a grounding wire, he snipped a flap through the wire.

One by one the men hurried through the hole. On the opposite side, the two officers shook hands, then motioned their men toward their targets.

55

MAJOR DEKE SLATTERY KNELT IN THE DARKNESS BE-
yond the missile complex. Hidden in the rocks nearby,
the SEALs and *spetnaz* were still recovering from the
difficult forced march over the mountain.

Farnsworth was soaked in his own sweat, and after
realizing the Russians spoke English better than he, was
again wondering why he had come on the mission.

"Interpreter's ass," he cursed softly as he scanned
the complex they had humped so hard to reach.

The complex was built into the side of a mountain.
An electrical fence, topped by ribbon-wire surrounded
the square-mile-sized military installation protecting the
entrance to the missile complex.

A single road passed through a main gate in a straight
line to the complex center, the commando's primary objective. On the sides of the roads, SAM missile bunkers
were buried deep in the ground. The crews were inside.
They wouldn't be a problem.

Not if everything went as planned.

Approximately thirty sentries walking in pairs with
guard dogs patrolled near the missile bunkers. Avoiding
the sentries and dogs would be critical.

At the mountain shielding the complex from air

strikes, a concrete bunker protruded from the base; embedded in the bunker was a huge steel door approximately ten feet high by twelve feet wide.

That was the main objective.

The door was closed. Slattery checked his watch. 0018.

Lieutenant Belenkov leaned to Slattery's ear. "What is your plan?"

Slattery pointed at the steel door. "According to intelligence, the door will open at 0030. That's when a bus carrying civilian workers to their custodial jobs arrives. The door won't open again until 0800, when the day shift arrives. We have to make our move at that time. The door can only be opened from the inside, from a control panel. We've got to get that operator before he seals the second door. If we miss the boat . . . we're shit out of luck and the whole operation is a bust."

"Why not have one of the attack planes fire a rocket through the door? Surely it could not withstand such an explosion," Belenkov asked the same question Slattery had asked.

"Because, once inside, there's another door. A bigger mother. It leads to the complex. The layout is similar to NORAD in the United States. The complex is designed so that an explosion at the first door will cause a landslide, sealing the second door from access by tons of rock. They can live for years inside that complex. Once it's sealed—we're fucked!"

Belenkov pointed at the two sentries standing near the steel door. "I will eliminate the sentries at the door." His voice sounded matter-of-fact, as though he were solving a math problem.

In a way he was, thought Slattery, who knew they only had one shot.

"Here. You'll need this little jewel," Slattery pointed at the four television cameras mounted over the front entrance. "This will jam the screens for only a few seconds. You'll have to move damned fast."

Slattery spoke into the boom mike of his communicator. "Red Cell Six . . . let's get busy. We have twelve minutes. *Spetsnaz*, you know what to do."

From the rocks overlooking the complex, the SEALs and *spetsnaz* moved quietly down toward where the fence ended abruptly against the mountain.

Belenkov and one of his soldiers continued on alone until they reached a point in the rocks approximately fifty feet above the concrete bunker guarding the entrance to the mountain.

"I hope they know their job," said Farnsworth. Beside him, one of the *spetsnaz* smiled evilly, then nodded. With the edge of his palm he made a cutting motion across his throat, then pointed at the two sentries.

Farnsworth understood. The youthful face of the *spetsnaz* officer betrayed his cunning, and deadliness, which they all watched moments later in a deadly display.

Slipping down from the rocks, Belenkov and the spetsnaz reached a position directly over the bunker. Carefully, they dropped onto the concrete roof, then slid on their belly to the edge. Four feet below an Iraqi soldier was lighting a cigarette.

The second sentry was standing at the corner of the bunker taking a leak.

Floodlights radiated from near where Belenkov raised his two hands. In one hand he held the jammer. In the other he held an automatic pistol. A long silencer was threaded into the muzzle of the Makarov 9mm.

Simultaneously, he pressed the jammer while pulling the trigger. A slight coughing sound was heard. The guard smoking the cigarette felt nothing. The bullet entered the top of his head, tore through his brain, nasal passages, his tongue, and exited beneath his chin.

He dropped like an axed bull.

At the precise moment Belenkov fired, the other *spetsnaz* fired at the soldier taking a leak.

The Iraqi looked up at the exact moment the *spetsnaz* fired.

Gripping nothing defensive except his shriveled dick, the Iraqi sentry pissed on his leg as the bullet tore through his right eye, then exploded from his skull behind his left ear.

It was over in seconds. The two commandos swung over the side, dropping to a crouch. They pulled the two dead bodies to the shadows and picked up their weapons.

Belenkov pressed the jammer, and waited to see if their plan had been foiled.

What he didn't know was that twelve feet away on the other side of the door, Amin Rushda, the console operator, had his eyes buried in an issue of *Penthouse* magazine displaying the firm, and very naked ass, of LaToya Jackson.

The magazine had been placed in Rushda's mailbox that afternoon by an Iraqi on the payroll of the KGB.

56

0030.

TWENTY-EIGHT MEN AND WOMEN PILED FROM THE bus in front of the entrance to the mountain. Like sheep, they huddled together waiting for the massive steel door to open. The bus pulled away, grinding its gears until it disappeared through the main gate of the installation.

Inside the mountain, Amin Rushda was still reading the articles when he heard a buzzer.

Looking at the television sets, he saw a soldier pressing the outside button. Behind the soldier stood the night custodial crew.

Rushda pressed a series of buttons. The first released the holding pins injected from the frame into the edge of the door. The second button released the pneumatic air lock inside giant piston-like arms sealing the door closed.

The third button activated the pistons, and the door groaned slowly opened.

Rushda slid the magazine under a pile of papers on his desk and walked to where the crew was entering.

Each person held out a buff-colored identity badge.

It was then that his eyes widened and he felt the sickening sensation in his stomach.

"Don't move!" A man dressed in an Iraqi uniform shoved through the crowd and was aiming a rifle at him.

Suddenly, the room filled with more soldiers, all of them shouting in English.

Rushda was not a brave man. But he knew the penalty that awaited. Without thinking he charged for the red button on the electronic control console.

A loud explosion filled the control room. Rushda felt himself flying.

A sharp pain erupted in his chest. He stared down at his suit. The white overalls began to turn red where a large hole was blown through the front of his chest.

Rushda slammed against the desk, spilling the papers onto the concrete floor. His eyes twitched, then turned slightly to the glossy cover of the *Penthouse* magazine.

LaToya Jackson stared emptily at him.

Two heartbeats later, Rushda's heart stopped beating.

Deke Slattery stepped over the dead man. In his hands he held a smoking M-16 assault rifle.

"Get these people the hell out of here," Slattery barked at Gunny and the other SEALs and *spetsnaz*.

The SEALs began pushing the terrified Iraqi's through the heavy door.

Slattery switched channels on his microphone and barked, "Red Cell Six standing on the dance floor. Strike up the band. It's time to rock and roll."

57

A LONG, ORANGE TONGUE OF FLAME ERUPTED FROM the RPG-7 rocket launcher mounted on the Soviet *spetsnaz*'s shoulder. Commander Harschenko watched the rocket streak toward the front window of the radar installation.

The explosion shook the ground; a red-orange fireball rose into the night, turning the blackness an eerie copper color.

"This is Commander Harschenko," the naval infantry commander said. "The radar installation has been neutralized."

In the barracks one-half mile away, sleepy-eyed soldiers began spilling into the streets as the wail of sirens suddenly filled the night.

A fat sergeant wearing nothing but his undershorts was the first through the door of the front barracks. He was carrying an AK-47 assault rifle.

The moment his feet touched the ground he heard an explosion; felt the shockwaves, then the tearing, skin-shredding torment of the ball-bearing projectiles that rent his body in a hundred places.

Lieutenant Dunstan pressed the second detonator, setting off another Claymore mine as the street began to fill with Iraqi soldiers.

From their position across the street, Dunstan and his four men were firing automatic weapons, setting off Claymores, and unloading RPG-7's and LAWs rockets into the front barracks.

At the two other barracks, two more four-man teams were doing the same.

Claymores exploded. Iraqi soldiers caught in the wave of ball bearings were cut down in mid-stride; some were waltzed backward on their tiptoes, looking like drunk ballerinas.

Blood flowed from the street to the barracks steps.

Dunstan switched channels on his communicator. "Red Wolf one . . . this is Force Recon. We're taking down the Ballroom. The radar installation is history. Get your asses in here. ASAP!"

"Hang on, son. We'll be there in six minutes. Start pulling your people back. You know where you're supposed to ride out the storm," replied Captain Boulton Sacrette.

58

FROM ONE HUNDRED FIFTY MILES TO THE SOUTH, the two squadrons of F/A-18 Hornets went to pure afterburner.

Six minutes later, Captain Boulton Sacrette led the pack from thirty thousand feet.

Switching on the FLIR, the forward looking infrared radar screen framed the first target.

At one thousand feet, Sacrette released a two-thousand-pound laser guided bomb from his starboard wing.

The bomb struck the operations center on the airfield, destroying the concrete building and what was left of the adjoining radar installation.

Pulling out of the dive, Sacrette banked right, came in on the deck and switched to his 20 mm M-61 cannons. A stream of red tracers roared from the gunports forward of the cockpit, joining the aircraft momentarily with an American-made Vulcan air defense gun position at the south end of the runway.

The gun position disintegrated in a matter of seconds.

Hauling back on the stick, Sacrette ordered, "Red Wolf one to all Red Wolves . . . hit your targets hard! Then join on me at Angels ten."

Sacrette hauled back on the HOTAS, pulling the Hornet into a steep climb.

At Angels ten Sacrette glanced out of the cockpit. Wearing the newly installed "cat's eyes" night vision goggles that made the Hornet an all-weather, all-condition, night-configured attack or fighter aircraft, he could see clearly through the blue haze caused by the lenses. Through cathode-ray tubes fed from the goggles, which looked like an instrument used by optometrists to check vision, the device projected the image picked up in the lenses directly onto the eye.

The airfield was being decimated. Fires from the barracks billowed as another Hornet delivered its deadly payload. The seven Vulcan air defense positions were eradicated within seconds as Hornet after Hornet dove onto the air base.

When the Hornets assembled on Sacrette, he gave the command to roll onto the second target. "Let's take the SAMs. Watch your asses. Go in low, stay low until you're clear of the target."

The Hornets dove from Angels ten in a matter of seconds. The missile bunkers were raising their payload when Sacrette's first bomb went down the throat of a SAM as it was preparing to fire.

The MK-84 2000-pound bomb turned the bunker into a flaming hole.

The fourth striker in the slot was flown by Lt. j.g. Robert "Rico" Rodriguez. Rodriguez set up his run from the west. As he neared the target, ground fire from a Vulcan stitched a string of deadly tracers through the night.

"I'm hit. I'm hit," Rodriguez shouted over the radio.

At Angels ten, Sacrette could see the Hornet pulling into a steep climb. Identifying his man was easy; the Hornet was spewing red fire from both engines.

"Get out, Rico," Sacrette calmly ordered. "Punch out. Now!"

In the cockpit, Rico and his RIO went through the pre-ejection checklist:

Feet extended to the rudders.

Heels flat against the deck.

Head firm against the headrest; chin elevated ten degrees.

Shoulders and back firmly against seat.

Elbows and arms firmly against sides.

Buttocks firmly against seat back.

Grip the ejection handle between your knees with thumb and index finger.

After Rico slowed the Hornet to one hundred eighty knots, Sacrette heard Rodriguez give the order: "Eject. Eject. Eject."

On the second eject command the RIO punched out.

Rico went on the third count.

Riding on igniting rockets positioned beneath the Martin-Baker ejection seat, the pilot and RIO shot three hundred feet straight up.

Seconds later the canopy began to deploy.

Sacrette lost sight of the men in the darkness.

"We've lost one," Sacrette spoke to Home Plate. Then he came back to the business at hand.

"Send in the troops."

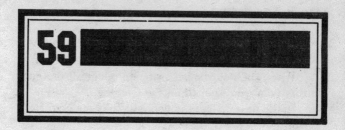

59

TEN MINUTES LATER THE MARINES LANDED AT THE missile complex coded Dance floor. Heavy H-53 Sea Stallions deposited their four-hundred-strong shouting, charging, firing human payload in front of the main gate.

Two Iraqi soldiers on duty dropped their weapons and raced off into the desert night.

Colonel Henderson led the troops through the gate. In a matter of minutes, fire teams were racing through the bunkers securing positions, taking prisoners, and killing the few Iraqi soldiers brave enough to resist.

When the installation was secure, Henderson ordered his men to take up a defensive perimeter around the complex.

Henderson took seventy-five men specially designated for the mission down the street leading to the entrance of the mountain's underground facility.

When Deke Slattery saw Colonel Henderson appear in the bright floodlights, he ran through the three button sequence to open the giant door.

"Semper fi!" said Slattery. He saluted Henderson and shook hands with the senior officer. After introducing Lieutenant Belenkov, the three men approached the console.

"Unbutton her, Major," Henderson ordered.

Slattery pressed the buttons unlocking the door.

When the door began swinging open, all the guns in the room were trained on the opening.

In the next instant the door was fully opened. Henderson slowly lowered his weapon.

Standing on the opposite side, in one of the many tunnels comprising the underground facility, Henderson saw a young woman dressed in a white laboratory smock.

She was standing there frozen with fear, staring wide-eyed at the marines.

In her hand was a half-eaten apple.

60

UNLIKE THE F-14 TOMCAT, WHOSE MILLION-DOLLAR-a-shot radar-guided Hughes AIM-54 Phoenix missile had a stand-off range of approximately ninety miles, the MiG-31 Foxhound's fourth-generation radar-guided AA-10 pulse-Doppler counterpart had less range.

Half the distance away, according to the blips on Zuberov's screen, were MiG-25 'Foxbats,' who carried the AA-6 "Aphid"—a third-generation, pre-AA-10 counterpart to the Phoenix. Zuberov knew the approaching Soviet-made fighters were at a distinct disadvantage.

Since the name of the game in aerial combat was getting off the first shot, Zuberov and his Foxhounds were primed and ready west of Baghdad.

From the rear seat, Captain Darkunin began "painting" the approaching MiGs with the radar. This was semi-active homing: radiation emitted from the radar hit the target, effectively "painting" the threat with radiation. The radiation then bounced back to the fighter. A missile was launched from the rail, and the sensors in the three-Mach missile tracked the threat by homing in on the stream of radiation feeding back off the threat.

The only requirement was that the pilot keep his radar on the approaching threat, keeping his nose pointed at the target. If the threat could evade by turning and running out of range or out of the envelope of the radar, the missile could become lost in space.

Which was why Zuberov waited until the aircraft were too far to fire their heat-seeking missiles, and too close to turn and run out of range of the Mach-busting radar missile.

When Zuberov fired the first missile, he knew the advantage was his.

With multiple-target capability, Zuberov was able to select five targets. Three more MiGs accompanying him in that sector did the same.

The fight was over before the Iraqis knew what hit them.

The blips disappeared.

That was when another set of blips appeared on the screen.

"Six targets approaching from the southwest," Darkunin said.

Zuberov studied the blips. They were flying in two-man formations.

Sixty miles. The point of merge, or when the battle could be joined, was coming up fast.

Decision time.

Zuberov moved to fire when the target moved into the radar envelope. That was when the sixth sense of the fighter pilot held Zuberov's finger off the trigger.

Instead, he quickly signaled the IFF identification friend or foe code. This was how two planes from tremendous distances could determine if they were friends. Or enemies.

As he looked at the targets, the six blips suddenly became boxed.

Zuberov switched to the crypto frequency and requested identification.

The voice that responded was that of an American.

"Red Wolf one to Red Star leader . . . ." said Captain Boulton Sacrette.

"Have activity on the Baghdad highway."

61

THE BAGHDAD HIGHWAY RUNNING BETWEEN THE MIS-
sile complex and the capital city snaked from the desert
through the mountains guarding Al-Nasra. The beams
from dozens of headlights could be seen from Angels ten
by Sacrette and the five strikers flying with him in formation.

"Fangs out!" Sacrette barked as he rolled the F/A-
18 Hornet over and started his bomb run.

Switching the weapons systems to the LAU-3/3A
2.7-inch rocket pods slung beneath the wings, Sacrette
"ripple fired" the nineteen rockets in the starboard
pod.

Through the bluish haze created by the cat's eyes
lenses, Sacrette watched a series of fireballs erupt on the
highway where the troop trucks were caught with nowhere to run.

The strikers bit and chewed at the convoy rushing
troops to the battle zone with devastating accuracy.

Within minutes the convoy burned from fore to aft.

"Red Wolf pack . . . knock it off." Sacrette ordered
the bombing to cease when he saw the convoy had been
destroyed.

That was when he heard Rhino's voice calling from the TAC CAP high above the desert at Al-Nasra.

"We've got gomers!" Rhino alerted the fighters flying cover.

62

RHINO HAD JUST COMPLETED REFUELING FROM AN A-6 when the E2-Hawkeye picked up targets moving low and fast from an army base near the Iranian border.

"Fangs out!" Rhino called to the carrier-based fighters.

"Like shooting fish in a bowl, Rhino," said Lt. Gooze Thomas, his RIO. The radar operator was watching the slower-moving blips move into the heat-seeking envelope.

"Let's start locking them up! Multiple targeting," ordered Rhino.

Focusing on the blips dancing off the HUD heads up display, Rhino began locking onto the heat sources of what could only be assault helicopters.

One by one the targets were locked up. Rhino began spitting his AIM-9L Sidewinders from the rails on the outboard wing pylons. Two heat-seeking Sidewinders shot from the Hornet.

"Fox two. Fox two." Rhino gave the call-sign, reporting that he had launched two Sidewinders.

That was when Gooze picked up on the Iraqi response.

"We've got heat. One missile incoming."

From six miles away one of the Iraqi helos had fired a missile of its own.

"They couldn't have picked up our six . . . our nose is on them. They must have locked onto skin heat." Gooze spoke calmly while watching the missile approach. Fuselage heat, while not as pure a heat source as engine exhaust, could still leave telltale signatures, especially during high-g manuevering.

"Hang on," Rhino called as he hauled back on the HOTAS. The Hornet went into a steep bat-turn.

"Two miles and closing," Gooze gave him the missiles distance.

"Going to ECM." Rhino hit the flare dispenser button. From the multi-ported chaff/flare dispenser in front of the port gear well, magnesium flares shot into the sky.

Drifting earthward on parachutes, the brilliance of the flares lit up the sky above the desert.

"One mile," called Gooze.

Rhino was about to execute another bat-turn when the darkness exploded into a flash of orange-red fire as the missile struck a flare.

Glancing to the HUD, the blips were gone. The fighters had reduced the threat to zero aircraft.

"Knock it off . . . Blue wolf. Return to TAC CAP," Rhino ordered.

The young pilot sat back in the seat. Perspiration soaked the skull cap beneath his helmet.

That was when he heard Gooze giggle over the radio. "Yo! Yo! Rhino! Are we bad to the bone!"

"We're bad to the bone, Gooze."

The young fighter pilots had just taken first place

in a game where medals weren't given for second place finishes.

They had seen the war dragon snap his tail and illuminate the horizon with lightning.

And survived!

63

0145.

SACRETTE EASED BACK ON THE THROTTLES AND raised the nose, flaring the Hornet ten feet above the runway at the airfield. Debris had been cleared by the Soviet airborne troops who dropped by parachute onto the airstrip within minutes after the battle began.

The airfield was under the control of the Soviets. He taxied to an area near the destroyed radar installation. Several hundred Iraqi soldiers sat on the tarmac, guarded by the airborne troops from the Soviet army's crack 106 Guards airborne unit.

Carrying AK-47's, the troopers wore their distinctive powder blue berets and blue striped t-shirts beneath their camouflage fatigues.

Sacrette found the Soviet command post and approached the commander, a Russian general.

They shook hands. That was when the CAG heard his name called in English, followed by a greeting used by only one type of the fighting elite.

"Captain Sacrette. Semper fi!" Lieutenant Clay Dunstan was walking toward him. A Soviet soldier walked at his side. A dozen men followed.

The SEALs and naval infantry *spetsnaz* had come

through the fray without a scratch.

Dunstan appeared tired, but swaggered with an arrogance Sacrette understood.

The men saluted. Sacrette shook hands with the Recon leader and Commander Harschenko.

"What's the sit-rep, Lieutenant?" asked Sacrette.

Dunstan pealed off the situation report. "The airfield is secure. The Iraqis caved in once the airborne arrived. Casualties are light. Ten killed. All Soviets. Soviet troop carriers are inbound for the extract. And there's something else . . . the Sov's picked up your two men who ejected. They're chilling out in a Sov aid station."

"Are they in good shape?" Sacrette was concerned.

Dunstan nodded. "Bruises. Shock. The rearseat man hurt his back. The Sov doc says his spine was compressed. They went for a helluva ride. You know that. I've never been there, but I understand it's an unforgettable experience."

Sacrette knew it was. Three things happened during ejection, none of them pleasant. The immediate effect was spinal compression. Some pilots shrank as much as one full inch and spent months in traction. Sacrette prayed that wouldn't be the case.

The second was shock: the body shut down all systems.

The third was bruising. Facial, and especially where metal buckles touched the body.

If their heads weren't secure against the headrest properly, their necks could snap like dry twigs.

If their feet weren't extended to allow a clean pull-back against the seat by the leg trolley, their legs could be sheared off at the knees.

After a "loud exit," the pilot and RIO often looked

like they had gone one-on-one with Mike Tyson.

"What about the missile complex?"

Dunstan grinned. "The SAM bunkers are destroyed. Marines have taken the installation. Colonel Henderson and Red Cell Six are setting the demolitions. Activity on the highway and in the sky is zero. I guess the Iraqis decided to write this one off. They took a real ass-kicking. They won't give us any more trouble. Captain Purcell said the Baghdad government had been told to sit on their hands unless they want the capital flattened."

Sacrette looked around at the devastation. "That would seem to be good advice."

"It appears to be working, Captain," Dunstan's tough veneer had faded into that of a young boy getting his first pony.

"You feel good, don't you, son?" Sacrette grinned as he asked the question, feeling pretty good himself.

"Yes, sir. It was my first combat." His voice faded a little, then he added, "I wasn't sure how I would react."

Sacrette clapped him on the shoulder. "Training breeds confidence, Lieutenant. Combat creates character. I guarantee this is a night you'll remember the rest of your life."

Dunstan laughed. His eyes were shining like two magnesium flares. "Semper fucking fi on that, Captain. Semper fucking fi."

Sacrette looked around. A Bell Huey 1-B helicopter was parked on the tarmac. He pointed at the helo. "Is that helo operational?"

Dunstan shrugged. "Let's find out."

A quick, but close examination of the Huey revealed an A-one helo. Sacrette then hustled to the aid station set up by the Sovs. He found Rodriguez and his RIO lying on a stretcher. A back frame was strapped to the RIO. Rodriguez was talking to a Sov airborne trooper wounded in the assault.

The Chicano pilot was trying to talk while reading from an English-Russian tour-guide dictionary.

Both of Rodriguez's eyes were black and blue. His helmet had blown off during ejection, but he stood and saluted, though slowly and obviously in pain.

That was all Sacrette needed to see to ask the question: "Rico, I know you're in pain, but I have to ask you something. A favor. There's nobody else who I can ask. And it's important. Damn important."

"Fire away, Thunderbolt," Rodriguez shifted his weight slightly to take the pressure off his aching spinal column.

"I want you to fly my aircraft back to the carrier."

64

"I PROTEST. YOU CANNOT DO THIS. YOU ARE COMMITTING an act of international terrorism." The words of the Iraqi scientist shrilled through the still air at the entrance to the missile complex at the mountain.

"So write your congressman, motherfucker. I'm damned sure going to write mine. Now get out of my face or I'll haul your skinny butt back inside that cave and strap you down on top of fifty pounds of C-4." CPO Diamonds Farnsworth was walking backward, chewing out the scientist while playing out a spool of detonation cord connected to demolitions inside the mountain.

Ten feet from the entrance he knelt and cut the wires from the spool.

Major Deke Slattery watched Farnsworth strip the wires of the det-cord and attach the naked ends to an electrical panel joining all the wires to a single detonator device.

"She's ready," Farnsworth said. He glanced to the wires.

Dozens of wires ran from the panel. At the other end, the det-cord was connected to a fifty-pound block of C-4 plastic explosives.

Each block was strategically placed to acquire maximum effect, including liquid fuel sources.

A marine nuclear specialist had determined there was no radioactive material in the complex. Only volatile liquid fuel sitting beneath a very large mountain.

"What about the civilians inside the complex?" asked Henderson.

"They've been cleared out of the area."

Henderson stared momentarily at the opening to the mountain complex. Then he nodded sharply and gave the order the mission had slowly worked toward. "Let's get back to the lima zulu. Then we'll see what this mountain's made of."

The marines of the assault wave had already pulled back to the LZ two miles from the installation where the H-53 Sea Stallions that brought them into combat was waiting to ferry them back to the Battle Group.

Thirty minutes later, the SEALs, Farnsworth, Henderson, and the *spetsnaz* were standing at a safe distance.

"Sir," said Slattery. He extended his hand. In his hand was a radio-controlled detonator set to the frequency of the detonator panel. "You get the honors."

Henderson looked at Lieutenant Belenkov. "Lieutenant, this has been a joint operation. Would you be my guest?" Henderson placed his index finger over the firing button.

Belenkov touched his finger to the top of Henderson's finger. "As you Americans say . . . fire in the hole!"

His finger pressed against Henderson's finger, activating the detonator.

The resultant explosion was no more than a whisper.

The Iraqi scientist appeared pleased. Noting his smug grin, Farnsworth told him, "Wipe that sassy-assed grin off your face. And watch that fucking mountain, Mohammad."

Seconds later the Iraqis grin evaporated as a low, slow rumble began to shake the earth.

Dust boiled from the opening that was there one moment, then gone the next.

The mountain seemed to split from the center down toward the desert floor. An ocean of rock moved toward the LZ, like lava from an erupting volcano.

The shock waves hit with the force of a Hornet taking off with afterburner power.

In the next instant, the missile complex at Al-Nasra was gone.

From the cockpit of the Huey, Sacrette watched the mountain disappear and said nothing. He couldn't find words to describe the awesome event.

"My God. The lid blew off." Dunstan breathed heavily. Four of his Recon team were sitting beside him. The two others were wounded and would be evacuated by the Soviets to an American base at Incirlik, Turkey, where the Soviets would refuel.

Sacrette steered the Huey to a soft landing near where the detonation team were jumping with joy.

He left the Huey in idle. Running low beneath the blades, he straightened once outside the range of the rotors.

Sacrette pulled Farnsworth and the Red Cell Six team off to the side. They talked for several minutes, then the SEALs went and collected their equipment.

Deke Slattery started for the Huey, followed by the Red Cell team, when he heard Lieutenant Belenkov call his name.

The *spetsnaz* followed their young officer, and in the glow of the light from the Huey, men from two nations, the fighting elite of those nations, stood staring at each other.

Then, like the rocks crashing into Al-Nasra, the American and Soviet commandos embraced each other one by one and said their farewells.

65

0600.

SABRY BAKR RODE GLORIOUSLY BETWEEN THE LEGS
of Yasmin Alabasi. Her face glowed; he could see she
was approaching climax. Moving beneath him in slow,
grinding circles, her hips suddenly thrust upward, nearly
causing him to dismount.

When she reached orgasm her screams echoed off
the ceiling, crashing back into Sabry's ears, spurring him
to drive faster. Harder.

As he approached climax he felt her body stiffen
and he thought she was going to climax again. Then he
looked down at her face. Her head was turned to the
side. Her large oval eyes were wide. What he saw wasn't
the ecstasy of sexual transport radiating from her face.

What he saw was terror.

Then he heard the metallic click from behind,
where Yasmin was staring.

Sabry's head snapped around. Then he stiffened
and his penis went flaccid within her sumptuous gate.

"Semper fi, Mohammad! I know the timing sucks,
so you two go ahead and finish your nut. Then both of
your asses belong to me."

Lieutenant Clay Dunstan was standing beside the

---

bed holding an automatic pistol. The silencer on the barrel was six inches from Sabry's head.

His camouflaged face was etched with a demonic grin.

Dunstan reached for Sabry's arm. Gripping the Iranian by the bicep, the Recon Marine pulled at Bakr.

That was when Yasmin's hips drove upward, spilling Sabry from her saddle.

Her hand flashed beneath the pillow, then reappeared. Clutched in her long slender fingers was an automatic pistol. It, too, was threaded with a silencer.

Both automatics coughed simultaneously.

Dunstan's bullet struck Yasmin in the throat, tore through the carotid artery and snipped her spinal cord at the base of the skull. Her head pitched back violently as the crushing impact of the .45 caliber Colt automatic shut down her central nervous system while she was trying again to pull the trigger.

She flopped sideways, then lay on the silk pillow. Blood streamed down her neck, forming a thick, rich pool between the cleavage of her breasts.

Yasmin's bullet caught Dunstan in the chest, driving him backward. Sabry pulled free, then started for the fallen Marine when he heard voices from beyond the door.

Several voices.

Sabry picked up the Marine's pistol and dashed toward the window. He sailed through the open frame bare-assed, hitting the ground in full stride as the room behind him filled with shouting men.

CPO Farnsworth was the first to enter, followed by Gunny Holden. The two black men split at the door. Farnsworth went to the window. Holden dropped beside Dunstan.

"Fuck!" shouted Farnsworth, who raised his weapon too late to fire at the fleeing Sabry, who by now was charging through the gate.

Gunny looked at Dunstan. The young officer's eyes were closed. A bullet hole was cut through his fatigues beneath the right pocket. The Marine SEAL spoke sharply into his boom mike. "Doc. We got one man down. Get in here. ASAP."

Slattery came through the door and paused. He looked at the fallen Marine. "Helluva way to start off a rescue mission."

The SEALs and Force Recon troops had entered the house unseen, under the cover of darkness, which was rapidly giving way to approaching daylight. The helo ride from the missile complex was a rock dodger, low, fast, with Sacrette riding the step ten feet above the deck.

By now Dunstan's Recon men and the rest of the Red Cell team were sweeping silently through the village, removing the threat of the few Iranians living there.

The mission was planned to move fast, hit hard, take no prisoners and show no mercy. A flat-out rock-and-roll SAS-type mission.

It was the way you dealt with terrorists, thought Slattery, who watched the young officer's eyes suddenly flutter open.

"Lay still, Lieutenant." Slattery heard Gunny speak softly.

Dunstan rose on his elbows. He looked down at the bullet hole, then grinned as he opened his fatigue jacket.

"We're tough, Major. But not that tough. I wore a little something extra." He tapped the bulletproof vest and pulled himself to his knees.

Slattery released a long sigh, then looked at the woman.

"Let's move," the SEAL barked to Farnsworth and Holden.

"What about the bare-ass?" asked Farnsworth, glancing at the bed.

"He'll be dealt with. Let's get the admiral."

As Farnsworth followed the two SEALs through the door he paused again, looking at Yasmin Alabasi. He shook his head in disgust. She truly was beautiful.

"Stone waste of some good-looking pussy."

66

HAKIM AL-SABBAH BAKR HEARD NOTHING BUT HIS footsteps as he walked from his spartan room into the hallway one flight above the dungeon. The six mullahs of the *Hafiza* were waiting as they waited for him each morning.

There was an unexpected smile on the face of the tall bedouin. He spoke to the Imam with particular joy. "The news this morning carried the reports of our brothers in Azerbaijan. Riots have broken out between Muslim Azerbaijanis and Christian Armenians. The Soviet government is sending troops. The revolution has begun!"

The old men clapped their hands loudly.

"Come," Hakim motioned up to the mosque. "We have a great reason to praise Allah."

The bedouin thought about the admiral starving to death in the minaret. A sadistic look spread across his leathery facial features.

It was then a noise from behind turned the six old mullahs' attention away from Hakim, who had started up the stone steps.

The piercing scream of the bedouin sounded the alarm. Head down, he ran charging toward the steps leading up from the dungeon. His halberd was poised outward like a knight jousting.

His eyes appeared insane.

"Infidels!" screamed the bedouin as he neared the first man up the steps.

CPO Diamonds Farnsworth squeezed the trigger of his M-16. Fourteen 5.56 bullets stormed from the muzzle, catching the bedouin flush in the chest.

The halberd shattered where the blade met the wooden staff. Flying lead and flying splinters exploded against the giant bedouin's chest, jerking him upright and to a halt. He seemed to be suspended in midair as his toes scruffed the floor and his body began flying backward under the momentum of the bullets.

From beneath their robes the six old mullahs pulled their revolvers, but the wall of steel now filling the narrow passageway had become a curtain of instant death.

Standing side by side, Slattery, Farnsworth, and Gunny Holden emptied their weapons into the old men until they were barely visible through the cloud of gunsmoke permeating the passageway.

"One got away!" Slattery barked.

"Like hell," replied Farnsworth, who leaped over the pile of dead mullahs with the speed and grace of Haven Moses.

From above, the CPO could hear the wild, maniacal scream of an old man. Slipping another magazine into the M-16 as he took the steps by threes, Diamonds wore the look of a madman.

The look of a man who had one purpose:

To commit cold-blooded murder!

67

ADMIRAL ELROD LORD HAD HEARD THE SHOOTING and was jerked from his semiconscious state. His lips were cracked; dry from the lack of water and the relentless sun.

He was barely able to turn his head to see who was charging at him, shrieking in a high-pitched voice reminding him of the screaming sirocco.

There was a blur. Then the image became clear as the crazed face of Hakim was clarified through his clouded brain.

Suddenly, there was an explosion. A rippling of explosions that turned the mosque into a cacophony of howls, shrieks, and gunfire.

Hakim's chest erupted through his robe. Blood and tissue spewed from the hole, splattering against the side of Lord's face.

Imam Hakim al-Sabbah Bakr, descendant of the bloodline of the "Old Man of the Mountain" pitched forward. His body lodged between the wall of the minaret and Admiral Lord's right leg.

Lord supported the old man's weight for a moment, trapping him there with Hakim hanging half in, half out of the minaret.

Hakim's head turned up to Lord's face. Their eyes met for a moment. Hatred flashed against hatred.

"'Revenge is mine...sayeth the Lord,'" whispered the admiral in a low, throaty voice.

Hakim's eyes widened as he felt Admiral Lord's body shift at the hip.

The supporting leg slipped away and Hakim pitched forward into the emptiness above the courtyard of the Monastery of Kims.

68

FROM THE COCKPIT OF THE HUEY, CAPTAIN BOULTON Sacrette had eyed the fleeing Sabry Bakr with a sadistic grin. Wearing nothing but a gold medallion, which was swinging wildly around his neck, the terrorist ran frantically across the rocky desert toward the Aerospatiale Puma helicopter.

Sacrette recognized the pistol in Bakr's hand. He recognized something else.

He recognized the look of fear on Sabry's face. The special fear worn by the pursued. Fear that stripped a man of all strength, rendering him into a mass of raw, running meat.

"You bastard," Sacrette breathed. "It's time the fiddler received his due." The CAG pushed forward on the collective.

The Huey came out of the sky like a diving falcon, screaming in a straight line toward the Puma.

"Not today, partner. Your flying days are over," Sacrette said to the image of Bakr.

Sabry Bakr heard the high-pitched whine of the Huey's engine. Looking up, he saw the helo painted in brown-and-loam desert camouflage pull up directly over the top of the Puma.

Sacrette hovered, then picked up the microphone and switched on the external loudspeaker.

"This is Captain Boulton Sacrette, United States Navy. Drop your weapon and put your hands behind your head. You will not be harmed."

Sacrette!

Sabry's mind snapped as the name brought back the day over the Gulf. The flaming Tomcat falling from the sky, plummeting his dead brother to his watery grave.

Sacrette!

The infidel he had killed a thousand times in his dreams.

Sacrette!

One of the men who was destroying the *Hafiza*.

Bakr's hand jerked straight out. The Colt began spitting the deadly projectiles.

The first bullet struck the windscreen. Spider-like webs appeared as a second struck.

Again he fired at the man he loathed.

"You son of a bitch! It's your call," Sacrette shouted.

Since the Huey didn't have any weapons, he was defenseless against the gunman.

Except. . . .

Sacrette went to full power, aiming the nose toward the gunman. Like an arrow, the Huey raced forward.

At the precise moment Sabry Bakr saw the pistol slide on the automatic lock-back indicating the weapon was empty, he saw the spear-like skid of the Huey pierce his chest.

He felt the punishing, penetrating agony as his chest split open when the skid impaled his body.

He felt himself begin to rise. His scream was lost in the prop wash and rotor slap.

Through the spider-webbed windscreen of the helo he saw the face of Sacrette. His mouth was spread in a broad grin beneath the visor of his helmet.

The helo banked sharply toward the monastery and he was over the courtyard. Through the pain he could see the admiral standing in the minaret, pointing down at a figure lying sprawled on the cobblestone court.

He tried to scream again as he recognized his father, but only blood spilled from his mouth.

Then he felt the Huey lower its nose and hover. He felt his body slide from the blood-slick skid.

He was falling.

And then . . . he felt nothing.

Epilogue

THE FLIGHT DECK OF THE USS *VALIANT* NEVER looked more beautiful to Admiral Elrod Lord. Bright shining aircraft were parked in neat, uniform rows. The sun danced from the surface to the deck, where thousands of sailors were jammed together as though they were returning to port.

Tears filled his eyes; through the wetness he looked at the back of the helmet of the man flying the helo, the man who had refused to leave him to the political process like the hostages in Beirut.

The man who had refused to leave him to die horribly.

He looked at the SEALs and Force Recon men packed tightly in the Huey and was reminded of the true meaning of courage, devotion, and fidelity.

He looked at the white-haired head cradled in his lap, felt the man's steady, but weakened grip, and understood that it is possible for enemies to become bound by a common hatred.

Air Marshal Lieutenant General Pietor Andreyevich Zuberov. The father of a man who shot down an American pilot Lord had treated like a son.

When the Huey touched down on the flight deck,

none of the sailors noticed the blood-stained skid, nor the bullet-shattered windscreen.

They rushed to the opened doors; hands reached inside, pulling the men from the helo.

One by one they were mounted on the shoulders of sailors who carried them proudly through a sea of cheering, shouting brethren whose emotions couldn't be restrained.

On human chariots of war, the SEALs, Recon Force, officers, and Russians were delivered to the main entryway leading to the island.

Captain Purcell stepped forward, his hand extended to Admiral Lord.

"Welcome aboard, Admiral." Purcell looked at Sacrette. There was a gleam in the exec's eye. A grateful gleam. One that signaled gratitude, relief. And slight irritation. "Captain Sacrette. Well done."

The men shook hands to the roaring approval of the sailors. Over the roar, Purcell had to shout to be heard by Sacrette and Lord. It was something he knew they would both want to know.

"The State Department has denied Colonel Scornicesti's request for political asylum. He's on his way back to Romania. I believe the Romanian government—and the people he helped brutalize—may give some thought to reinstating the death penalty. Just this one time."

"Couldn't happen to a nicer guy," Sacrette replied. Then the CAG saw another officer approach.

Domino pushed his way to Sacrette. The Brooklynite stuck out his hand. "Welcome back, Thunderbolt."

"No hard feelings?" asked Sacrette.

Domino shook his head. "I needed some time to

think things through. I'll be getting the best medical attention money can buy. I'll be back, CAG. You need me. The navy needs me. Hell, man. I'm a two-million-dollar fighter pilot."

Behind Domino stood Rhino and Gooze. Like the rest of the pilots of the carrier, they stood there grinning like monkeys.

Doc Holwegner pushed his way through the throng to the admiral, who was weary, haggard, but wearing the smile of a newlywed.

"Admiral, let's get you to sick bay," Doc Holwegner motioned to two corpsman.

Admiral Lord shook his head. He pointed at the four Russians. "Take care of these men, Doctor. I'm in pretty good shape." He looked around at the smiling sailors. "I'd like to stay here for a few minutes."

As the corpsman led the Russians away, General Zuberov walked weakly to Admiral Lord. Rather than say what he felt, he lightly tapped and scraped his message on the admiral's chest.

Spasee'ba.

Thank you.

No one understood except the two combat commanders.

That was when the Soviet air marshal heard a voice call to him in Russian. A voice from the crowd calling, "Poppa."

Major Sergei Zuberov stepped through the crowd and approached his father. The two men embraced, and as the son began leading the father away, he paused beside a man who had sent him a note that only said, "I'm going after your father."

They said nothing. In words. They shook hands. A

long, affectionate clasp of hands once sworn to the other's destruction.

Zuberov looked at the sky. The sun was brilliant. The sky was blue, clear. A forever sort of sky.

In the distance the sound of a commercial jet departing Al-Kuwait airport rumbled faintly.

"It is a good sky for flying," said Zuberov, who caught sight of the jetliner as the L10-11 rose above the Gulf.

"Yes. A good sky for flying. A pilot's sky."

Zuberov released his grip. As he started away he paused, and said to Sacrette, "It has been a most interesting day . . . my friend."

Sacrette knew the words didn't come easy; honesty never does between enemies.

The CAG ran his hands roughly over his face. Then he grinned that Sacrette grin. The eyes hooded, but not in anger; his mouth parted into a smile. "A very interesting day . . . my friend."

The jetliner noise grew louder, and in the next instant was over the two fighter pilots standing alone on the flight deck of the carrier.

And then it was gone.

Taking with it some of their hatred.

A former paratrooper and combat veteran of Viet Nam, Tom Willard holds a commercial pilot's license and has lived in Zimbabwe and the Middle East. He now lives in Grand Forks, North Dakota.